DANCING AWAY WITH MY HEART

A SMALL TOWN SOUTHERN ROMANCE

KAIT NOLAN

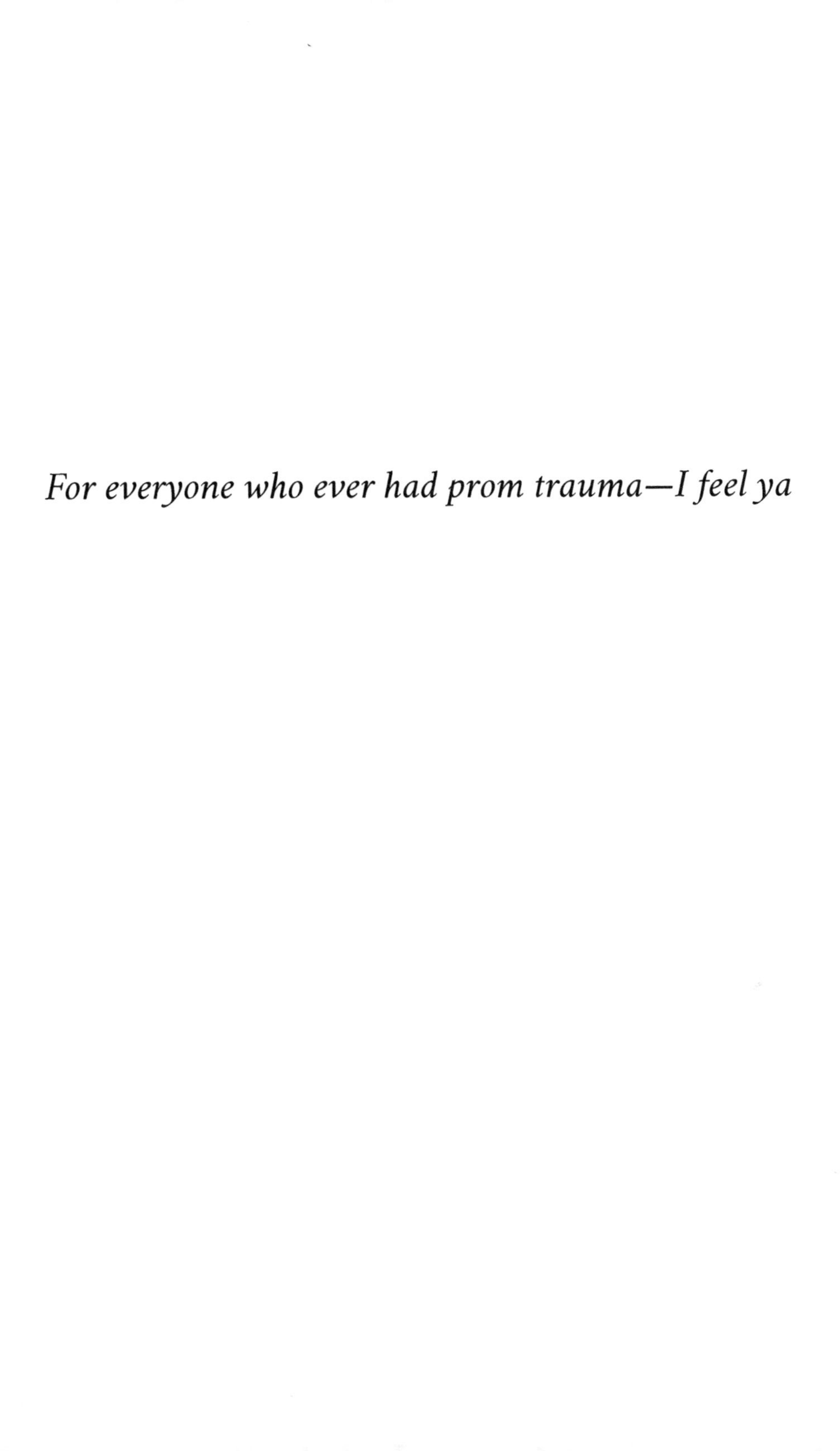

For everyone who ever had prom trauma—I feel ya

Dear Reader,

This book is set in the Deep South. As such, it contains a great deal of colorful, colloquial, and occasionally grammatically incorrect language. This is a deliberate choice on my part as an author to most accurately represent the region where I have lived my entire life. This book also contains swearing and closed door pre-marital sex between the lead couple, as those things are part of the realistic lives of characters of this generation, and of many of my readers.

If any of these things are not your cup of tea, please consider that you may not be the right audience for this book. There are scores of other books out there that are written with you in mind. In fact, I've got a list of some of my favorite authors who write on the sweeter side on my website at https://kaitnolan.com/on-the-sweeter-side/

If you choose to stick with me, I hope you enjoy!

Happy reading!

Kait

*T*he light was perfect. A thin layer of clouds diffused the early evening sun, casting a warm glow over the Wishful town green. All along Main Street, flowers bloomed from carefully-tended planters and trees leafed out in a vibrant chorus of spring. People strolled or sat, enjoying the breezy, upper-sixties temperatures and soaking up sunshine on what was arguably an absolutely perfect spring day. Lexi's shutter finger twitched, and she wished she'd grabbed her camera when she'd gotten out of the car. She wanted to linger in the golden hour, while everything seemed just a little bit magical. But she was on a mission. Still, she turned her face into the cool caress of the wind and gloried in the sweet scents of azaleas and jasmine.

"Why, Lexi Morales, is that you?"

The delighted drawl snapped Lexi out of her reverie. She blinked at the older woman, who sported a huge, shellacked helmet of hair in an *I Love Lucy* shade of red. Back when she'd taught tenth-grade English, she'd been known to change it as frequently as other women changed purses. There'd been a pool going on the color of the month. The winner got a whole dozen of their candybar of choice. Lexi had ended up with a lot of Snickers that year.

"Mrs. Landon."

Mamie Landon beamed, opening her arms and automatically pulling Lexi in for a pillow-soft hug. "How are you, sugar? I didn't realize you were back in town."

Knowing there'd be no escaping without at

least a short visit, Lexi resigned herself to a delay. "Well, it wasn't a planned thing. My mom had a fall and broke her ankle."

One hand went to Mrs. Landon's ample bosom. "No! I hadn't heard! Why, I need to bring by a casserole. What happened?"

"She was trying to clean out the gutters and the ladder slipped. She fell right off. Clean break. She's okay, but I'm here to help out for a few weeks until she gets back on her feet." And to take care of a myriad of other things around the house that her mom had no business trying to do on her own.

"It's such a blessin' that you could get away that long from your job."

Lexi smiled a little. "My boss is pretty accommodating."

"What is it you're doing now?"

"I'm a photographer." She'd finally been able to afford to sign a lease on studio space in Austin. A lease she wouldn't be able to pay if she didn't figure something out for income while her mom recuperated.

"That's marvelous, darlin'. Seems like almost every memory I have of you from high school, you had a camera in your hands. You and that Warren boy. Used to be thick as thieves."

The faint smile froze on Lexi's lips. Yeah, she didn't really need a reminder of "that Warren boy." She'd made avoiding him without being rude an art form over the past decade.

"He's a photographer now, too," Mrs. Landon continued, oblivious to Lexi's discomfort. "Runs a studio right here in town. Did you know that?"

"Yes ma'am, I'd heard that. We keep up a little bit on social media." It was all she'd been able to stomach. But she was back in town for longer than a weekend now. She wouldn't be able to steer clear of him forever.

A bright flash of color drew her attention to the fountain at the opposite end of the green. A young couple, decked out in formalwear, grinned at each other, posing in front of the post-Civil War monument that had given the town its name. Over the years, people had come from all over to make wishes in its waters. According to Lexi's mother, the new city planner had capitalized on that colorful history over the past few years in a marketing campaign to increase tourism. Lexi supposed duping the masses with foolish hope was as good a reason to draw people to town as any, but she knew better. The fountain certainly hadn't granted her wish all those years ago.

Her gaze skimmed from the couple further back, searching out the photographer and hoping it would be some proud parents wanting to capture their kids in all their finery. But it wasn't parents.

"Oh, there's Zach now! It's prom night for the high school, so I figured he'd be out and about somewhere."

Of course, it was prom tonight. Because this walk down memory lane wouldn't be complete without that insult to add to her very old injury.

Lexi's skin went hot and prickly, and a whole murmuration of starlings performed aerial acrobatics in her stomach. She hadn't seen him in years. Not really. She could barely see him now at this distance, but she recognized his crouch with a camera lifted to his face. A face that now showed signs of a scruff he hadn't had when they were in high school. His sun-tipped brown hair was a little long, the way she'd always liked it. He was all dialed in to his subjects, calling out orders for posing, keeping them relaxed and comfortable. He'd always had a gift for that, where she'd had to work for it. She'd always, always preferred shooting any subject that wasn't people. But she'd gotten over it. Needing to eat was a powerful motivator, and weddings, engagements, and portraits were her bread and butter.

Mrs. Landon took Lexi's arm and began towing her down the sidewalk toward him, one hand lifted in a wave, despite the fact that his back was to her. Any second now she was going to sing out "Yoo hoo!" and draw his attention.

Lexi dug in her heels. "No, Mrs. Landon, it's bad form to interrupt a shoot. They'll lose the light. I'll catch up with Zach later."

As she watched, the boy dipped his date back in dramatic fashion. Laughter carried over the green, and Lexi felt a pinch somewhere in the vicinity of her heart. The bite of jealousy was fast and surprisingly vicious.

Oh my God, really? You are a grown-ass woman. Are you really jealous of a couple of seventeen-year-olds?

The unfortunate truth was yes. She hated prom season and all the reminders it brought. While she wasn't sure how she was going to make ends meet the next several weeks, she'd been thrilled to escape more of the shiny, happy teenagers and their parents, who approached the occasion with nearly as much seriousness as a wedding.

"I'm sure he'll be just delighted to see you."

Lexi doubted that. They barely qualified as

friends anymore. "I'm sure it'll be good to catch up later. I've got time, after all." Sucking in a breath to calm her racing pulse, she managed another smile. "Listen, Mrs. Landon, it was so wonderful to see you, but I need to be getting on. Mama sent me into town to pick up mochas and brownies from The Grind."

"Of course, of course. You tell your mama I said hello now, you hear?"

"Yes ma'am, I will."

"I'll bring that casserole by later this week!"

"We surely appreciate it. Thanks again." Before Mrs. Landon could start in on any other subject, Lexi ducked away and hustled across the green to the coffee shop.

As she stood in line, she managed to get herself under control. It was stupid, really. She'd known she'd see him eventually. Wishful didn't even have a population of six thousand people. Over the past decade, she'd managed to limit those random encounters, coming home only rarely for weekends and sticking close to the house, rather than out and about.

Her mother, God love the woman, had never asked for details about why Lexi no longer wanted to see the boy who'd been her best friend from the first summer before she'd started at Wishful High School, back in ninth grade. Lexi had hoped that time would dull the ache of missing him and the burn of embarrassment she felt every time she thought of him. But it hadn't. Not yet, anyway. So, she'd have to bite the bullet, take control, and arrange to see him on her terms. After she'd had a chance to get her head screwed on straight.

"Lexi?"

At the sound of the familiar male voice behind her, she closed her eyes.

Crap.

ZACH STOOD JUST inside the entryway to The Daily Grind. All thoughts of the clients he'd just finished with, and the large Zombie Killer with caramel he needed to fuel the late night of editing ahead, spilled out of his brain. The next few seconds unfolded like a series of still shots, each moment captured clear in his mind as she turned. In each one, she transformed a little bit more from the girl he remembered to the woman before him. The woman he'd barely seen in a decade. Every blink was another shutter click, storing away mental images, cataloging the differences between then and now. She was still petite, but the compact body in his memory had added more than a few curves. The rich, brown waves of her hair were longer now, pulled back in a low tail at her nape.

But it was her. It was Lexi.

Joy burst like a barrage of flash bulbs in his brain. But there was something else there, too. A tightness in his chest he didn't expect. Like he couldn't quite catch his breath. An inability to look away from those melted chocolate eyes. Had they always been this deep and piercing? Her lips curved as she smiled that familiar, Lexi smile, and the thing in his chest loosened.

Before he could check himself, he'd closed the distance between them, scooping her into his arms, and lifting her off her feet in a fierce hug. "Damn, it's so good to see you!"

It took a second to register that she wasn't hugging him back. Realizing he'd overstepped some boundary they'd never had before, he set her down, finding himself strangely reluctant to release her, as if she'd disappear in a puff of smoke the moment he stopped touching her. Lexi Morales hadn't been a day-to-day part of his life since they'd graduated high school, but he'd never stopped thinking about her. Never stopped wondering how the hell they'd gone from easy, everyday friends, to the keep-up-on-social-media distance they had now.

As soon as her feet hit the floor, she took a step back, and he noticed that smile he'd missed so much was a little strained around the edges. "Hi, Zach."

Shit, should he apologize for invading her

personal space? Not knowing what else to do, he shoved his hands in his pockets to keep from touching her again. "I didn't know you were in town."

Glancing at the line, she edged closer to the counter. "Only just. My mom broke her ankle."

Zach frowned. How had he not heard about that? He tried to keep up with Mama Morales since Lexi was more than a few hours away in Texas. "That's awful. Is she okay?"

"Yeah. But she can't manage on her own right now, so I'm here for a few weeks to help out." There was a flash of…something in her eyes before they shuttered.

Zach realized he'd seen that before, when she'd started to retreat at the end of high school. He hadn't known what to do with that back then. She'd never hidden what she was thinking or feeling before. It had always been one of the things he'd loved about her. He knew exactly where he stood with her. When she'd started pulling away, he'd thought it was a phase. She'd always been an intensely private person, so when she'd put up boundaries, he'd respected them instead of demanding she tell him what was going on. He'd thought she'd snap out of it. She hadn't. High school had ended, they'd gone to different schools, and somehow…they'd never found their way back to the friends they used to be. He'd been able to keep up with her on social media. Maybe that had made him feel like they were still closer than they actually were because he was painfully aware that he couldn't read her right now.

He didn't know where this standoffishness was coming from. Okay, maybe she hadn't responded the way he wanted when he'd reached out online. They'd both been busy with their respective lives. It happened. But maybe it was more than that. Did she have something going on that he ought to be concerned about? As far as he was concerned, they were still friends. If she needed support for something, he wanted to be there for her.

The line moved, and they took another step toward the register. "Is everything all right with you being here that long?"

The question seemed to take her aback. "What?"

"It's just, you seem less than thrilled about it."

Two spots of color bloomed in her cheeks. "It's not that. I love my mom. It's just a long time to be away from my life in Austin."

"And does that life include a significant other?" He hadn't seen her post anything about a guy on social media, but she didn't post about a lot of things.

Lexi snorted and sounded more like herself. "Like I have time for a boyfriend while I'm getting my business off the ground."

Zach felt an absurd sense of relief at the news. Why should it matter if she had a boyfriend or not? It wasn't like a guy would take her away from him. Life had done that already. And things had never been anything more than platonic between them.

"So it's work you're missing?" This was probably safer territory. They'd always been able to connect over photography.

"Well, it's hard to book jobs not knowing exactly when she'll be healed enough for me to get back."

He'd been lucky in his business. Byron Bridges had retired the year Zach graduated from college. Coming home to take over his studio had been a no-brainer. There'd been a built-in client-base, and as the only professional photographer in town, he tended to stay busy year-round. So busy, he didn't have time to pursue his other interests. But maybe, since Fate had sent Lexi back his way, he'd get a little reprieve. And maybe he could help her out along the way.

"Work with me while you're here." The words were out before he could think them through, but he wouldn't have taken them back. He missed working shoulder-to-shoulder with her in a dark room or on digital proofs. No one understood the lure of being behind the camera the way she did.

Those melted chocolate eyes blinked. "I'm sorry?"

"Since Byron retired, I'm the only gig in town, so I've got more business than I can handle. There's a waiting list, and there have been some jobs I've had to turn down because of time constraints. I know it's not growing your client list for Austin, but it'd surely keep some income flowing while you're here."

Why did she look so stunned at the offer? They were friends. Or damn it, they used to be. He wanted that back. Spending actual time together would give him the chance to reestablish their friendship in a way he couldn't online. He'd known he'd missed her, but he hadn't realized how much until he'd seen her again. He needed her to say yes to this.

"Your clients want to book you. Your skills. Your style."

"They want good pictures," he corrected.

"Most aren't that fussy about who takes them, and you're every bit as good as I am. It'd be great to have someone to refer them to that isn't an hour or more away. You brought your gear, didn't you?"

The look of vague insult almost made him smile. "Of course I did."

"Then it's a win-win for us both." *Please, say yes.*

She fidgeted, and he was sure she was trying to come up with some excuse. "Well, if you truly don't mind and don't think they'd mind, I'd certainly appreciate some referrals."

Zach held in his whoop of relief. "Of course I don't mind. What are friends for? I'd love to get to really catch up while you're here. It's been ages."

Again that…something flashed across her face, but she stepped up to the counter to place her order. By the time she'd finished chatting easily with the barista and paid, he'd already mentally rearranged things in his studio to accommodate another photographer and started a list of ways to remind her of all the reasons they'd been friends in the first place.

Grabbing the paper bag and tray of coffees, she turned toward him, smiling again. "I'd love to catch up while I'm here. But later. I promised Mom brownies and a mocha, and I already ran into Mrs. Landon on the green, so I've taken longer than I meant to."

Squashing the disappointment that they couldn't start that catching up now, he pasted on his own smile. "Of course. Give your mom my best. And come on by the studio tomorrow. I'll give you the grand tour. It'll be nice to share it."

"Looking forward to it." She lifted the bag in a sort of wave and headed out the door.

As he watched her go, Zach couldn't quite shake the feeling that she was running. With luck, he'd eventually suss out why.

CHAPTER 2

*B*ecause she needed to burn off a little more nervous energy before she got back in her car, Lexi took the long way, skirting by the fountain. It actually ran now, which was more than could be said for it back when they were in high school. A tiny, foolish part of her wondered if that was why that long ago wish hadn't come true.

I wish Zach would see me the way I see him.

He hadn't. Ever. The truth of that had been too painful for her to cope with, so she'd put distance between them, hoping time would heal the wound. Apparently, it had. Getting through that whole interaction had taken less acting than she'd expected. She *was* legitimately happy to see Zach. He had, after all, been her closest friend for many years. She didn't hate him or wish him any ill will. She just wanted to turn off the feelings that had turned on for her their senior year and go back to only being buddies. Things had been so much simpler then.

For a fleeting moment, she considered dropping another coin in the fountain, updating her wish. Could you even do that? But ultimately, she let it alone. She'd spent all these years building up what it would be like to see him again. She'd always been so afraid to look him in the eye and see the knowledge of her feelings for him. Maybe to see that he thought it was sweet, or cute, or that she was just a little bit pathetic. And then she'd have to die from the abject mortification. But it had been...fine. Turned out Zach was still as clueless as he had ever been. Sure, she'd felt a little awkward, but not the dry-mouthed, tongue-tied, heart palpitations she'd expected. He was just...Zach. Perhaps it was time she admitted they were all grown up and she'd moved on.

Thank God.

Clearly, he still thought they were friends, like he didn't even notice the distance she'd put between them. The contrast to her own perceptions was jarring. But maybe this was a good thing. Maybe she could put her old crap away and they could find their way back to being real friends while she was here. Wouldn't that be something? The idea of it had her smiling as she let herself into the little gray house with the bright turquoise front door.

"I was beginning to think you'd been kidnapped by a drug cartel."

Lexi glanced at the TV, where the protagonist of her mom's current favorite telenovela was engaged in a dramatic stare down with the son of the cartel's head. "Ricardo totally figured out Maria's undercover, didn't he?"

Her mom gestured expansively toward the screen, wincing a little as her movement shifted the ankle she had propped on a pillow. "Yes, but he doesn't know *why* yet."

Crossing the small living room, Lexi set the coffee and brownies on the table in front of the sofa before sinking cross-legged to the floor. "She's going to have to trust him if she has a prayer of finding out what happened to her sister."

Eyes never leaving the show, her mom grabbed one of the mochas. "He might turn her over to his father." Her tone was caught somewhere between dread and excitement. Leandra Morales was a fan of the drama. As long as it stayed on the screen. In her own life, she just wouldn't have it, divorcing Lexi's father on the discovery of his infidelity, despite her Catholic upbringing. That had all happened when Lexi was fourteen, and was how she and her mother had landed in Wishful for a fresh start.

"Never gonna happen. He's been secretly in love with her from the beginning." Lexi actually had no idea if he was or not, but she'd watched enough telenovelas growing up that it seemed a safe bet.

On the screen, Maria's eyes glimmered as she insisted she could explain, that it was all for the sake of her little sister.

Lexi tapped a finger against the lid of her cup. "Called it!"

They lapsed into silence for the last few minutes of the episode, which ended with the star-crossed lovers in a passionate embrace. It was ridiculous and over the top, as most telenovelas were. And still her heart gave a little twinge. When was the last time she'd had somebody kiss her like that? Hell, when was the last time she'd been on a date at all? She'd done her share of dating in college, though nobody had been serious. Since then she'd been far more focused on finding a way to make a living with her art. There'd been a couple of guys she'd seen more than once, but nobody worth making the effort for a real relationship. In truth, she didn't think the right relationship would feel like work. So, either she simply hadn't found the right guy, or she was fooling herself.

Leandra clicked off the show and pounced on the brownie. "Now, tell me what took so long."

Lexi twitched her shoulders and bit into her own brownie. "It's Wishful. You know there's no such thing as coming back to town without having to chat with everybody and their brother."

"Which everybody did you run into?"

"Mrs. Landon. She's planning to bring a casserole over, by the way."

"That's nice of her. Who else?" Per usual, her mother's sharp eyes missed nothing.

Lexi wondered if maybe she had a blinking neon sign above her head. She kept her tone as casual as possible. "I saw Zach."

A delighted smile bloomed on Leandra's face. "Oh good! He always asks about you whenever I run into him. I know he's been wanting to see you." She didn't say it, but the implied question of why Lexi hadn't made an effort to see him on her previous visits home hung in the air between them.

Lexi knew better than to bite. And she knew that her mother wouldn't push. She'd never pushed Lexi to handle things with Zach any other way but how she wanted, even when it meant that Lexi had moved three states away. Not that she'd ever admitted he was the reason.

"Well, he'll be seeing a fair bit of me while I'm home. He's offered me a job. Sort of. He's got more business than he can handle—nice problem to have, right?—so he's going to make some referrals."

"That's wonderful, *mija,* and a big relief to me. I didn't want to ask you to come for so long—"

"Don't be silly." She was all her mother had.

No way was she shirking that responsibility. "Of course I was going to come. And we're lucky I have the flexibility to do exactly that."

But the relief of probably getting some kind of work while she was here couldn't be overstated.

"How do you feel about spending time with him again?" Leandra's eyes were full of far too much sympathy.

Lexi had never told her the whole story, but she'd always suspected her mom knew anyway. She'd worn her heart on her sleeve back then. Before she'd learned how to armor up and shove those more tender feelings in a deep, dark basement room of her heart.

"I don't know. It's good to see him." In those minutes she hadn't been freaking out, she'd drunk in the sight of him. The easy smile, those shoulders—broader now—that tapered down to narrow hips, the crinkles around his blue-gray eyes…

When she didn't continue, Leandra nudged her knee. "But?"

Lexi mentally shook herself, choosing her words carefully, so she didn't reveal too much. "We have a lot of history. Mostly good. But I'd be lying if I said I wasn't worried it'll be a little weird." Then again, the weird was only ever on her side. She was the one who'd changed. Zach seemed just as blissfully unaware now as he had been in high school. There'd clearly been no epiphany on his part about why she'd up and almost disappeared.

Whatever. She was a successful adult, with a full life elsewhere, who was no longer crushing on her best friend. His obliviousness didn't matter.

"Friendships are like the tide. They ebb and flow. You've been at an ebb with Zach for a long time now. Maybe now the tide is turning."

"Maybe," Lexi conceded.

She just hoped she could keep her head above water.

Zach minutely adjusted the level of high-lights in the image on the screen, but his attention wasn't on the smiling teenagers in the shot. Another glance at the clock confirmed it was nearly five. Lexi hadn't shown. He was starting to think maybe she wasn't going to. Maybe it just wasn't a good day for this. But if that were the case, why hadn't she let him know?

He could call her mom's house. It wasn't like he didn't still know that number by heart. But somehow it felt desperate to call her up to say, "Hey, where are you?" when they hadn't even set a formal time to meet. He wasn't desperate—not exactly—just…antsy. And he couldn't figure out why. There was some part of him that worried she'd disappear on him again. Or maybe that he'd imagined yesterday's encounter entirely, just because he'd missed her. Until he'd laid eyes on her, he hadn't realized how much. And that was… crazy. Right? Not the missing her part, but this sense he had of needing to hang on. Maybe it was just his subconscious prodding him not to let things go back to this polite distance they'd had the last several years. She'd pulled away so gradually, somehow he'd missed it. What kind of a dick did that make him that he hadn't noticed until it felt like it was too late to do anything about it?

Well, I'm doing something about it now.

A chime sounded, indicating someone had opened the door. He sprang out of the chair and bolted for the reception area.

Lexi stood in the front office, a camera bag slung cross-body as she looked around at the gallery of photos on the wall. The sight of her was like the sun coming out, banishing the vague shadow that had hung over his day. He didn't bother trying to tame his grin.

"Hey! I was beginning to think you weren't going to be able to make it."

"Sorry. I had to go by Brides and Belles to pick up the latest alterations. Mom insists she doesn't need her ankle to do them, and neither Babette nor I could talk her out of it. Then it took a while to get her settled in her sewing room." She shoved her hands in the back pockets of her jeans, an old tell he recognized. He didn't want her to feel awkward here with him.

"No problem. I was just doing some editing. Come, have the grand tour. It'll only take about five minutes."

He led her back to the studio and watched her take everything in with those dark eyes that missed nothing.

"It looks so different from when we interned with Byron."

"After he retired, I had the guys come in to help me paint from top to bottom. And as soon as I could get rid of the early eighties era furniture, I did. I didn't need too much. I do way more on-location shoots than studio work."

They picked their way over the snaking cords of flash stands and around reflectors. "Same. It's how I could get away with not having a proper studio all this time. I never liked working with backdrops."

"They have their place, but there's no substitute for natural light." He showed her the prop room, full of everything from an assortment of chairs and artificial plants, to empty picture frames, to the buckets and baskets he often used for newborn shoots. And he took great delight in showing her the dark room.

She turned a circle in the small space. "You actually still do film?"

"Not as often as I'd like, but from time to time. There's just something about doing the development yourself, you know?"

"Oh yeah. I have fond memories of the time we spent in the dark room back in high school."

Coming from anybody else, that would've been a double entendre, but from Lexi it was nothing more than the truth. The dark room had been about confidences and confessions, and plenty of laughter. They'd had some of their best conversations there.

"Maybe you'd like to try your hand at it again, while you're here."

Her lips curved. "Maybe I would. For now, I'd like to see more of your portfolio. See the kind of thing your clients are expecting."

"I'll show you mine if you show me yours."

She nodded and followed him into his office. Zach pulled up his digital portfolio and nudged her into the seat, trying not to loom as she clicked through.

"I thought I'd know more people."

"You've been gone a long time. Things change, even here in Wishful."

Lexi twitched her shoulders and didn't look at him. "True enough."

Damn. He hadn't meant that as any kind of recrimination.

"Reed Campbell is getting married?"

Zach peered over her shoulder at the engagement photos he'd taken. "Got married last fall. Cecily is a blue blood from Connecticut, but we forgive her for being a Yankee since they're besotted with each other."

"It shows. She's lovely."

Lexi continued to scroll, commenting on others she recognized who'd gotten married or had kids. Eventually she sat back, a strange vulnerability to her expression. "It feels weird."

Zach leaned against the desk, crossing his arms. "What does?"

"I don't know. It's like they're all grown up, and I'm still playing at this adulting thing."

"There's no deadline on when or if those things happen. They're not for everybody."

She angled her head to study him, her full lips quirked in a sardonic smile that was a shade more of the Lexi he remembered. "You? Is there a prospective Mrs. Warren on the horizon?"

It was a casual and obvious question to ask, but he was oddly relieved to admit, "Nah. The dating pool here is shallow, as you well remember. I'm enjoying my life exactly as it is." And if he'd been feeling the pinch a bit with his friends starting to get married, that was natural. Wanting to change the subject, he slid off the desk. "So show me what you've been working on."

She logged into her online portfolio and they traded places. Where his stock-in-trade was traditional weddings, family shoots, and senior portraits, her work was far more artistic and varied. He clicked open a folder titled "Home." The gallery loaded, one image after another showing the coast in miniature. Zach opened the first thumbnail, a sunset shot of the iconic Biloxi lighthouse that had miraculously survived Hurricane Katrina.

"You went back."

"It was time," she said softly. "I went back on the ten-year anniversary."

The anniversary of when her family had lost everything. Their home in Bay Saint Louis had been entirely washed away. Without the money or will to rebuild, they'd relocated to Houston, Texas, crammed into a little apartment for a few years, before her parents split, and she and her mom had moved to Wishful. All these years later, few people outside Mississippi remembered that New Orleans hadn't been the only city hit. Even when it had happened, The Weather Channel had referred to the space between New Orleans and Mobile as "a land mass" rather than an actual state, for which they'd been mercilessly mocked by other networks. The fact of it was, the Mississippi Gulf Coast had been obliterated. Lexi clearly remembered. And yet the photographs she'd taken chronicled the things that had survived, what had been rebuilt.

He understood what that trip had meant to her. Facing that loss. "I'd have gone with you."

Her hand squeezed his shoulder before falling away again. "I know. I needed to do it alone."

Once they'd done everything together. Zach didn't understand where or why things had changed.

Not trusting himself to bring it up, he kept scrolling, admiring the breadth and scope of her talent. He was impressed, and a bit envious. "I'm a little jealous of all this."

"Why?"

"I'm good at what I do, and I enjoy it, but there's a sameness and expectation to traditional photography. What you've done here? This is art."

"I'm going to disagree that your traditional photography isn't art, but there's nothing stopping you from exploring other things, too."

"There's not much time for that with everything else on my plate. Bills to pay, and all that."

"Art doesn't always pay. Or hasn't yet, for me. Not a living wage, anyway. That's part of why I started my own studio. I have do the one to enable the other."

"I'm hoping I can do a little branching out and experimenting with you here."

Her lips curved. "Still into weather photography?"

Before Zach could reply, her phone rang.

"Excuse me." Stepping back she answered, "Hey Mom," and wandered out of the room.

Zach kept clicking through her galleries. She'd done everything from landscapes to abstract macro studies and everything in between. And then he hit on the folder of boudoir shoots. It was a style of photography he'd never thought of doing. There was an unavoidable intimacy between subject and photographer, and he couldn't fathom it not being awkward with his friends and neighbors. But Lexi clearly had no issues on that front. The pictures were sexy and tasteful.

One particular sequence of black-and-white images captured his imagination. The model was clearly nude, but nothing could actually be seen. It was all sensual curves, the suggestion of intimacy. Tastefully erotic. He could almost feel the softness of that skin beneath his palms. The next shot captured the same model from behind, rising from tangled sheets. There was no lover in view, but her mussed hair implied a night of passion. The angle showed only her back and the top curve of her hip. In the next one she slipped on a cardigan long enough to cover the essentials. He could practically hear the whisper of fabric as it settled over her. The one after that, she stood at a window, her face turned away, but every line of her lovely body suggesting wistfulness, as if she were waiting for that imagined lover to come back. He clicked to the next, a waist-up shot where she was turned partly toward the camera, the gap in the sweater showing a tantalizing suggestion of breast as she glanced back over her shoulder. And his breath backed up in his lungs.

It was Lexi.

Had she done these herself? Or had that mystery lover implied by the composition been responsible? Why did the idea of that squeeze a fist in his chest? She was an adult. A single, incredibly attractive adult. Of course she'd had lovers.

"Sorry about that."

By some miracle, Zach managed not to fall

out of his chair. But he didn't manage to school his face.

"What's wrong?"

I've just been perving on my best friend.

"Nothing." Before she could circle the desk, he closed out of the folder and randomly selected something else. "Just admiring your work. You're really versatile."

You're really beautiful. How did I never really notice that before? Those semi-erotic images of her were etched into his brain now. He couldn't unsee that, couldn't go back to seeing her as just Lexi.

She frowned at him as she crossed over, so he tried to change the subject and mentally started reciting the focal lengths of his entire collection of lenses to get his arousal under control. "Was everything okay with your mom?"

"Oh, yeah. She was just letting me know that Babette dropped over with dinner. I think she wanted me to know I don't have to be on duty for a while."

He closed the browser entirely and stood. "Does that mean you're free for the night?"

"I suppose it does."

"Then let's get some dinner and take a walk down memory lane."

Maybe by the end of it, he'd manage to shift her firmly back into the friend column.

CHAPTER 3

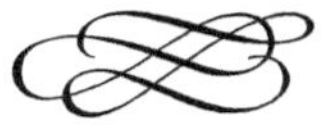

"The first time I had a camera in my hands—a real camera—was out here, on a night much like tonight. Do you remember?"

Lexi didn't look at Zach in the driver's seat, her gaze trained instead on the small crowd milling around a bonfire on the banks of Hope Springs. "Of course I remember."

It had been her camera. A gift from her father that was supposed to be some kind of apology for not keeping it in his pants and destroying their family. Completely new in town, starting over *again,* with two whole months before she began high school, her mom had dropped her at a similar bonfire, with a promise to come back for her after an hour.

"I need you to try, mija.*"*

Lexi could still remember the panic clawing up her throat at what felt like being thrown to the wolves, but she'd gotten out of the car, clutching the camera like a lifeline and a shield. And instead of walking up and introducing herself as her mother intended, she'd skirted the group, studying them through the viewfinder. She'd framed and tested shots, adjusted settings, eventually losing herself in the process and forgetting she didn't really want to be there.

And then Zach had walked over.

"Can I try?"

She'd eyed him with suspicion. The camera had been expensive. Who was this *gringo* with the open face and easy smile? But he'd won her over with his relentless good humor and general *niceness,* until she'd let him try the camera out, taking a picture of her.

"I still have that picture of you at home," he said, proving his thoughts were running along the same lines.

Now she did look over, something warm blooming in her chest at his sentimentality. "You're a lot better now than you were at fourteen."

"Yeah. But I think it's good to remember where we came from. C'mon. Everybody's waiting."

There was something odd to his tone and his expression, but she didn't manage to put her finger on what before he was climbing out of the car. She thought he was going to head on without her, but he stopped a few feet away and turned back, a hand outstretched as it had been that night all those years ago. Riding on nostalgia, Lexi slipped her camera bag over her head and placed her hand in his. Zach's fingers closed warm and sure around hers, and she tried not to read anything into it.

There hadn't been more to it then and there wasn't now. He was just a physically affectionate guy. Always had been. But she was aware of every millimeter of his skin where it touched hers.

"Look who I found!" Zach dragged her into the light of the fire.

"Lexi!" A familiar brunette scrambled out of a camp chair and launched herself across the distance.

Laughing, Lexi absorbed the enthusiastic hug. "Hey, Avery! It's great to see you."

"Hail, hail, the gang is officially all here. Welcome home, *chica*." Leo Hamilton scooped her neatly off her feet.

His twin brother lifted an arm, with a grin she hadn't forgotten. "Eli, if you even think about putting me in a headlock and giving me a noogie, I swear to God, I will show you every bit of the self-defense I learned in college."

"Spoil-sport." But his blue eyes twinkled as he said it. "Welcome back."

She was passed from hug to hug. Jace Applewhite. His cousin, Jessie. Reed Campbell. And then came the introductions to the significant others. Avery's fiancé, Dillon was a rangy guy who somehow looked like a cowboy despite the khaki shorts and t-shirt. Lexi wanted to get a shot of that profile from beneath the brim of a Stetson. She recognized Reed's wife, Cecily, from the photos she'd seen in Zach's portfolio. She was even more stunning in person.

"It's so nice to meet you," Cecily gushed. "Zach's talked so much about you."

Lexi arched a brow and glanced at him. "He has?"

Zach only shrugged. "You feature prominently in most of my high school stories."

"They used to be joined at the hip," Jace said.

"Oh, did y'all date back then?" This came from a leggy blonde she didn't recognize.

"No." The word came out too fast, too sharp, and Lexi hoped they'd attribute the flush in her cheeks to heat from the fire. Fixing a smile on her face she managed a passable laugh. "That would've been ridiculous."

"I thought you were joking."

The long ago words echoed through her heart with a stab of pain just as fresh now as it had been when it happened.

Over and done. Get it together. Stuffing her emotions way down deep, she forced herself to relax and roll on with the conversation, facing the blonde. "You're clearly new since high school."

Jace slid an arm around her waist and beamed. "Lexi, I'd like you to meet Tara Honeycutt, the love of my life."

The pair of them oozed happiness and contentment, the kind that couldn't be faked for pictures. Jace had always been so damned nice, she couldn't resent that, even if she did feel a stab of envy. "Pleased to meet you, Tara." A diamond flashed in the firelight. "When is the big day?"

"Weekend after next. Will you be in town? You should absolutely come," Jace insisted.

"Of course, I'd be happy to come."

"Actually, I wanted to talk to y'all about that." Zach snagged a Coke from the cooler and popped the top. "Lexi's in town for a few weeks, so I wanted to see how y'all might feel about bringing her on to help with wedding photos."

Okay, this was not exactly what she'd imagined when Zach had offered referrals. She'd expected client meetings and formal presentations, not putting everybody involved on the spot, last-minute.

"I'm a groomsman," he explained. "I can cover all the posed shots, but you and I both know there's no substitute for an active photographer during the ceremony. I could make it work, but..."

"It wouldn't be the same," Lexi finished. She couldn't fathom trying to be *in* a wedding *and* shooting it.

"Oh, could you?" Tara shot an apologetic

look at Zach. "I know you said you could handle it, but I've had reservations."

"Completely understandable," Zach soothed.

Good thing she'd packed for work, just in case. "I'd love to help. Just let me know where and when."

"Awesome!"

Avery offered her a beer. "So you're here for a few weeks? Are you back for the reunion?"

Lexi bought a moment, twisting off the cap and taking her first pull on the longneck. "The reunion?"

"You know, our ten-year class reunion," Leo prodded.

She'd done her best to block out the fact that it was even happening. The absolute last thing she wanted was to go back to high school, even for one night. Not even with these people she'd once been so close to. "No, I'm not in town for the reunion. I'm helping out my mom. She broke her ankle."

There were the predictable exclamations of concerns and offers to help, which Lexi neatly brushed off. It had been just her and her mom for so long, she wasn't accustomed to taking much in the way of help. Plus, it was a point of pride that they'd managed on their own after her father's infidelity.

"Still, it would be a shame for you not to come if you're still here," Avery insisted. "You'd get to see everybody from high school."

"I'm seeing everybody from high school I actually want to see right now," Lexi pointed out.

"Flattery will get you everywhere," Jessie declared, toasting with her own bottle. "But the point, dear girl, is dressing up."

"Dressing up?"

"The whole thing's ending with a grown-up prom. How cool is that as a way to flash back to the good ol' days?"

They all clearly had vastly different memories of high school than she did. Flashing back to the worst stretch of her teenage life was not how she wanted to spend an evening or even a minute. She'd done it often enough over the years without having a practical reenactment of the event.

"I'm not much one for dressing up." And she wasn't. The number of times she'd willingly worn a dress in her adult life for non-business purposes could be counted on one hand. She was a tomboy. Always had been. Jeans and Chucks and an assortment of vintage t-shirts were her uniform. What business did she have trying to be someone she wasn't? That hadn't ended well for her before.

"Seriously? Your mama is, like, the most talented seamstress in town, and you don't take advantage of that?" Avery asked.

Lexi's fingers tightened reflexively on the bottle in her hand. "Nope. She despairs of me, I promise. But it doesn't make me like dressing up any better."

Jessie opened her mouth, presumably to continue her campaign, but Zach interrupted. "Leave her be. She's never liked dances."

It was the truth as far as he knew, and her one attempt to change that had blown up in her face.

"How can you not like dancing?" Jessie asked.

"I like *dancing* just fine. I just prefer to be comfortable while doing it. No pointy-toed shoes that break my feet. No panty hose. None of the torture device trappings that go along with dressing up."

Leo pulled out his phone and stabbed a few buttons. Music spilled out of a speaker by the cooler—something with a beat that made her hips twitch. "No time like the present."

More appreciative than she could express, Lexi tipped back the rest of her beer, then set the bottle aside. "You, Mr. Hamilton, are on."

OVER THE NEXT FEW HOURS, Zach watched Lexi unwind, losing herself in music, memory, and more than a little bit of alcohol. Why not?

He was driving, and he suspected she cut loose little enough in her day-to-day life. It was the reason he'd brought her, hoping to coax her into relaxing and remembering the easy friendship they'd all shared for years. That and he'd wanted to spend time with her. As if in one night he could make up for years of distance.

But the night hadn't done for him what he'd wanted. It hadn't reminded him that they were friends. Hadn't neatly nudged her back into that box and locked any kind of a door. Because he couldn't take his eyes off her. Couldn't stop soaking in the sound of her laughter and the way the firelight illuminated that gorgeous, bronzed skin. Skin his hands itched to touch, to see if she was as soft as those pictures had made her look. She'd let her hair down. The heavy mass of waves spilled down her back, bouncing as she swayed to the beat. What would they smell like? Feel like against his fingers? They'd danced together in packs, as friends were known to do. But he'd never danced with *her.* He found he wanted to.

So, of course, he kept his ass parked in a camp chair on the other side of the fire, well out of touching range, since he'd lost his damned mind.

"Earth to Zach."

He blinked, realizing Leo had been talking to him and he hadn't heard a word. "What?"

"Dude, what is up with you?"

"Nothing." *First line of defense, always denial.*

"I'm calling bullshit on that." Leo looked across the fire to where Lexi danced with the other girls to somebody's Girl Power playlist in a sort of tipsy, tribal display of the modern feminine. "It's not exactly like old times, is it?"

Uncomfortable with where that question might lead, Zach jerked his shoulders. "We're not in high school anymore."

Leo lifted his beer. "That's for damned sure. You never looked at her like this in high school."

"Like what?" But he knew.

"Like you want to take a bite out of her. When did that happen?"

Zach rubbed a hand over his face, as if he could scrub the image of scraping his teeth down the long, lovely column of her throat out of his mind. Wonderful. Now he had new fantasies to add to the ones she'd inadvertently planted in his brain herself. But it hadn't just been the boudoir shots. Things had felt different the moment he'd laid eyes on her in The Daily Grind. "Hell if I know."

"What are you gonna do about it?"

"Do?" He skewered Leo with a look. "Not a damned thing. She's one of my best friends. I'm not going to fuck that up."

Leo studied him for a long moment, like he knew the truth—that Zach and Lexi hadn't been best friends for a long time. And maybe he did. Maybe they all knew what he hadn't been able to admit to himself.

"So you're just going to…what? Hope this goes away?"

Yeah, that'd be good. He'd go home, get a good night's sleep, and when he woke up tomorrow, he'd be sane again, and they could resume working together with that easy, uncomplicated friendship they'd always had. "Sure. Why not?"

Leo snorted. "Good luck with that, brother."

"What's that supposed to mean?"

"Just that there's a reason the opposite sexes rarely make it long-term as platonic friends. Somebody's feelings always change. Hell, I had a front-row seat to that most of my life with my brother and Autumn, and look where they ended up."

Married with a baby and blissfully happy.

"That's different." Everybody knew Judd and Autumn had been in love with each other since they were six years old.

"I'm just sayin'." Leo stood, finishing off his beer. "I need to be getting on. The work day will start way too soon."

"You good to drive?"

"Yeah. That was just my second over several hours. I'm good."

Zach rose too, thinking he should probably cut Lexi off before she had to face Mama Morales with a hangover. Nobody wanted that. She was belting out an enthusiastic, if slurred, rendition of "Titanium", using a wine cooler as a microphone.

"Okay, Miss Bulletproof. Time to go."

"Awwww." She broke into a spate of Spanish he didn't understand.

Oh boy. She only retreated to her first language when she was really tired, really emotional, or, apparently, well on her way to drunk.

"Your mama's gonna kill me."

Giggling, she held a finger up to her nose. Zach could only presume she'd been aiming for her lips, miming keeping a secret. He wondered if he'd be able to sneak her into the house and pour her into bed without Mama Morales finding out. Only one way to find out. He began herding her toward the car, a process encumbered by the fact that she kept running back to give everybody big, sloppy hugs.

"I missed y'all so much!"

Zach was glad she'd remembered that much, at least.

By the time he leaned over to buckle her safely in the passenger seat, he knew there wasn't a chance in hell of retrieving her car from the studio tonight. At least it gave him another excuse to see her tomorrow. But maybe after all this he wouldn't need excuses. Maybe they'd fall back into things the way he wanted.

Tipping forward, she pressed her face into his throat. "You smell good."

Zach froze, feeling half the blood in his body drain south at the feel of her lips against his skin. His fingers fumbled the seatbelt. Yeah, their old friendship was definitely not what he was wanting right now. Electing not to comment, he fastened the belt and shut her inside.

Just get her home.

She hummed the whole way to some playlist in her head. It took him until he parked in her driveway to recognize what it was.

"Are you humming that mix CD I made you freshman year?"

She rolled her head toward him against the seat. "It's one of my favorites. You're one of my favorites. Always were."

"You're one of my favorites, too, Shutter-bug. C'mon. Let's get you inside."

He told himself he only kept his arm tight around her because she was stumbling, but he was aware of every inch of her body moving against his on the way to the house. The door wasn't locked, for which he was grateful. A single light burned from the entryway table. Moving past it, he carefully navigated her down the hall to her old bedroom. When she started to giggle, he shushed her.

"Do you want to get us both in trouble?" he whispered.

Lexi pressed her face against his arm and shook with silent laughter.

They made it into her room without incident—a miracle. He reached for the desk lamp, relieved it was still exactly where it had been in high school. Depositing her into the chair and shrugging off her camera bag, he studied her flushed face. Oh yeah, he should have cut her off one or two sooner.

"Don't go anywhere. I'm gonna get you some water and aspirin."

The glasses were still in the cabinet above the dishwasher. He filled one and found the painkillers—they'd moved since high school— then returned to Lexi's room. It felt weird being here at night, in the dark, trying to be quiet while her mom slept down the hall. Like they were doing something illicit. Which was ridiculous. Naked thoughts notwithstanding, he was just putting his drunk friend to bed. Then he'd leave.

Lexi was trying to pull off her shoes when he came back.

"I've got that. Here, drink this."

She took the aspirin and guzzled down the water. When he was sure it was going to stay down, he bent to remove her shoes.

"Help me up," she demanded.

When he did, her hands went to the button of her jeans.

"What are you doing?" he croaked.

"Not sleeping in jeans, silly." Before he could protest further, she unzipped them and began wriggling them down those curvy hips.

Oh dear God in heaven.

Her bikini briefs were black. Of course they were. They were seared into his brain before he could tear his eyes away to fix them on something, anything else. The erection he'd been fighting since the seatbelt came roaring to life.

"Need a hand, Zach."

She'd managed to get the jeans to her ankles but didn't seem to be coordinated enough to step out of them without falling over. Taking a firm grip on his control, he reached out to steady her while he gently worked her free of the denim. One foot.

"Okay, now the other," he ordered.

She braced a hand on his shoulder and began to lift her foot.

He didn't know how it happened. One second he was bent in front of her, detangling her from her jeans, the next they'd tumbled onto the bed, with him sprawled atop her, between her bare legs. And now he knew for sure that her skin absolutely was as soft as it looked.

Lexi didn't giggle. She didn't shove him off. She stared up at him, those melted chocolate eyes going darker and darker as they dropped to his mouth. He couldn't stop himself from mirroring the move, gaze tracing over her parted lips. They were full and rosy and *right there*. What would she taste like? He could feel her quickened breath against his skin, and every cell in his body screamed to close that tiny distance and kiss her.

On a sigh she closed her eyes. Beneath him, her body went lax.

"Lex?" he whispered.

Her only answer was a soft, wiffling snore.

He didn't know whether to curse or send up a prayer of thanks.

Moving as carefully as he could, Zach eased off her. He tugged off the jeans still dangling from one ankle and draped them over the chair. Then he folded her, burrito-style into the comforter on the bed. He couldn't resist stroking a hand over the hair spread over her pillow. Silk. At least now he knew that, too. But as he quietly turned out the light and let himself out of the house, he didn't think the knowing would do a damned thing to stop this inconvenient attraction.

CHAPTER 4

"I'm so glad you're here to help me with this. I've been wanting to clear out this closet for ages, and I just can't ever seem to get to it."

Lexi had no idea what had possessed her mother to want to clean out the guest room closet today. Possibly it was subtle punishment for the mild hangover neither of them was acknowledging. Or maybe she really did just want to take advantage of having Lexi as free labor. Either way, Lexi dutifully returned to the closet, grabbing up another armful of clothes from the rack and hauling them out to the bed.

"I'm thinking a lot of this can just go straight to the donation pile. I don't think either of us has worn this stuff in going on a decade."

"But so much of it is in such good shape. I could change up some of the lines, add some embellishments, update the style…"

Lexi lifted her brows. "Mama, just because you *can* remake this stuff doesn't necessarily mean you *should*."

She understood how hard it was for her mother to just let go of something that was still good, still useful. Leandra had grown up poor, the daughter of Puerto Rican parents who'd moved to Mississippi for a new start. New clothes had been a luxury, and her skill with a needle had meant she'd been able to update whatever they'd had. That same skill had been pressed into use in the years after Katrina, when they'd been rebuilding from nothing. But things weren't that dire anymore, and Lexi didn't want to see her mother pushing herself too hard outside her work for Brides and Belles.

"You're supposed to be resting, remember?"

"I am resting. You're doing all the heavy lifting."

Rolling her eyes, Lexi disappeared back into the closet for the next load. And she found it in the back, still draped in plastic. The Dress. The exquisite, perfect dress her mom had made for prom all those years ago that had never been worn. She could hardly bring herself to touch it. God, she'd wept over this dress and everything it had represented. Her one and only attempt to change things. At being brave and striking out into the unknown. And she'd been thoroughly smacked down by the Universe. Lesson learned. Risk all in business but never in matters of the heart. Maybe she needed that reminder as she and Zach worked their way back to friendship. Because friendship was the only thing that had ever been on the table.

Bracing herself, she grabbed the dress and carried it into the guest room. "Why is this still here?"

"It's a gorgeous dress. I couldn't see getting rid of it. I thought maybe you'd eventually want to wear it for something else."

It was gorgeous. Some of her mother's best work. But she could never wear it. "I don't live the kind of life that calls for formalwear, Mama."

Leandra clapped her hands in inspiration. "You could wear it to the class reunion! Babette told me there's a formal dance. Several of your former classmates have been into the store the past few weeks looking at dresses."

"I'm not going to the reunion."

"Oh, but why not? You'll be in town. I'd think you'd want to hang out with all of your friends."

"I can hang out with them without going to the reunion."

"It seems a shame to waste the opportunity to wear the dress."

"You and I both know this wouldn't fit me now. I'm not as small as I was in high school."

"But you could—"

"Mama!" Lexi sucked in a breath, immediately sorry for her harsh tone. "Please let it go."

Leandra held up her hands in a gesture of peace. "Okay."

Lexi couldn't quite look at her. "You know how much I appreciate what you put into this dress. I'm sorry I never got the chance to show off your handiwork."

"I know, *mija*." The gentle understanding in her tone made Lexi want to burrow into her mother's arms to cry as she hadn't let herself do then.

The doorbell rang.

Lexi gently laid the dress on the bed. "I'll get it." Firmly locking away old hurts, she headed for the front door.

That old wound gave a throb when she

found Zach on the front porch, hair still damp from a shower, looking clean and fresh and annoyingly hangover-free. But it was mostly drowned out by the quick burst of pleasure at seeing him again. She could endure the discomfort for this.

"Hi."

"Morning." His eyes skated over her, assessing.

With her messy bun and yoga pants, Lexi felt like something the cat dragged in. She resisted the urge to tug at the hem of her t-shirt or pat at her hair. There wasn't a damned thing to be done about her appearance and it didn't matter anyway.

"How's the head?"

"I've had worse. I guess I have you to thank for that." She had fuzzy memories of him getting her home, making her drink water and take some aspirin.

Something in his eyes darkened and for just an instant Lexi's chest went tight. Like she'd seen that look before in far more intimate circumstances. Which was utterly ridiculous. She must've dreamed it. Still, she couldn't stop the flush of heat that swept down her body or the yearning to sway into him.

His lips lifted. "What are friends for?"

She had to be imagining that strain around the edges of his smile. What would he have to feel awkward about?

He held out one of two to-go cups from The Daily Grind. "Here. This will help what's left of your headache."

Automatically, she took it, backing up to let him inside. "What is it?"

"Hangover cure. We don't ask Cassie what's in it. We just say please and thank you."

"In that case, thank you." She took a cautious sip, pleased when the dominant flavor was still coffee. "Who's the other one for?"

"Your mom. I know she's got a fondness for mochas."

"Zach Warren, is that you?" Leandra's voice echoed down the hallway.

He grinned and the weirdness of the moment passed. Lexi could feel them recalibrating, getting back on even keel again.

"Yes ma'am!"

"Come on back here and give me a hug."

Lexi tipped her head. "Guest room."

She followed him back, relieved to have a few moments to get herself under control.

Zach skirted the bed and bent to give her mom a solid squeeze. "Hey Mama Morales. It's great to see you. I come bearing gifts."

"Seeing your pretty face is gift enough." Leandra patted his cheek, eyes sparkling.

"Oh, well then I guess I'll drink this mocha myself."

"Mocha?" Her mother reached out with grabby hands, making him laugh. "You are a good boy, Zach."

"I certainly try." He glanced over the chaos. "What's going on here?"

"She's got me cleaning out the closet." Using the excuse of making a place for him to sit, Lexi shifted some clothes on top of the dress so he wouldn't see it. "Have a seat."

She didn't wait to see if he did, just went back into the closet and resumed her work. "So what actually brings you by this morning, other than a mission of coffee?"

"I thought we could discuss strategy for shooting Jace and Tara's wedding and then go get your car."

Right. Her car was still at his studio. She hadn't even thought of that yet this morning. Which just went to show how little her brain was firing.

"You were such a dear to put her to bed last night," Leandra said.

Lexi choked on her next sip of coffee. "Put me to bed?"

The tips of Zach's ears went red. "You, uh, weren't exactly steady on your feet."

Lexi opened her mouth to say...she had no idea what. She'd been drunk and he'd put her to bed. And her mother had apparently been awake to notice. Great. Figuring silence was the only acceptable response, she started to drink more coffee, then froze, the cup an inch from her mouth. She'd been in her t-shirt and *underwear* when she woke up, wrapped in the comforter like a human burrito.

Oh God, did he undress me?

With reluctant horror, she met Zach's gaze. As if he could read her mind, he gave a small shake of his head. Lexi didn't know if that made it better or worse. There was a tightness in his jaw, a seriousness in his eyes she didn't know how to read.

They were just starting to get back to where they used to be, and she was glad of that. She'd missed him, more than she cared to admit. So she would put whatever that imagined look was out of her mind. It wasn't attraction. It couldn't be. Because that wasn't who they were to each other, and she didn't want to screw up their rekindling friendship by giving in to the seduction of hope.

Needing to get out of the room, away from her mother's far too observant eyes, Lexi straightened her shoulders. "Right, well, it seems we have some work to do. Mom, can we finish the closet later?"

"Of course, *mija.* I'll sort through what you've already pulled out."

"Great. Zach, give me fifteen minutes to shower and change clothes, then we'll go have a strategy session."

Without waiting for an answer, she strode out, hoping they didn't realize she was running.

"THIS IS the official twenty-minute warning. Everybody finish getting dressed and get your butts down to the orchard for the ceremony. Got it?" Evan Applewhite spread a look over the assembled groomsmen who sprawled in various states of undress around the barn apartment at Applewhite Farms.

From his position by the window, Zach

snapped a picture, capturing the mix of stern and repressed laughter.

"We've got it, Dad." Jace shrugged into his vest. "Any last words of wisdom?"

Evan crossed to his son, reaching up to straighten Jace's tie.

Click.

"Never go to bed mad. She's always right. And don't ever take her for granted." He squeezed Jace's shoulders. "You already did the hard part. You found the right one."

"She's one in a million."

Click.

"I better get out there before your mother starts to fret. See you on the other side."

Zach adjusted a few settings as Evan departed, relieved that he could simply relax and be a part of the wedding party, taking prep shots of the groom and groomsmen getting ready. Lexi was serving the same function over at the big farmhouse, where the bride and her attendants were dressing. She'd had a much earlier start to the day, going with the women to the salon, documenting hair and makeup, and the thousand other details that went along with properly capturing the bride on her wedding day. Zach could have done those shots, but there'd be an intimacy another woman could capture that he simply couldn't.

He'd never worked with a partner before. Not really. He had the occasional intern to help tote equipment or swap out lenses, but he hadn't ever had a true second shooter. Knowing she was here as backup dropped his stress level considerably. Thanks to Lexi, he wouldn't have to rely on timers or worry about any kind of prospective malfunction during the ceremony. He wouldn't have to stress about working with someone he didn't know well. Jace was one of his best friends. He didn't want to risk having anything but stellar shots of his wedding. Lexi would give him that.

Over the past week, they'd spent time together every day, talking wedding strategy, scouting the location, and even tag-teaming a couple of smaller shoots. Their working relationship was seamless, and they'd slipped back into their friendship like a favorite pair of jeans. In many ways, it was like she'd never left. It was easy to imagine that this is how things would have been if she hadn't.

Except she had left. He'd gotten used to being without her. Now that she was back, he couldn't quite seem to put her back in that Lexi-shaped hole in his life. Because favorite jeans or not, she wasn't just friend Lexi. She was woman Lexi. That unfamiliar attraction hadn't done anything but amp up in the days since the bonfire, and Zach had no idea what to do about it.

"Hey Warren, you're falling down on your job." Eli's taunting voice cut into his thoughts.

"What?" Zach blinked, focusing on the room-at-large.

Jace and his soon-to-be brother-in-law, Austin, were clearly in the middle of a Moment. Automatically, he lifted his camera and fired. In seventh grade and gawky with it, Austin was serving as best man. Zach knew the two had gotten tight over the past few years Jace and Tara had been dating, and he hoped he hadn't missed anything important.

Leo nudged his shoulder. "Maybe keep your head on the wedding instead of your pretty partner."

Despite his low voice, of course everybody heard.

"You've got a thing for Lexi?" Reed asked.

"You mean you didn't see him practically drooling over her last weekend at the bonfire?" Eli asked.

Oh hell. Was I that obvious? "I'm not dignifying that with a response."

"Evading the question. That counts as confirmation," Reed said.

"Oh for the love of—We all need to get down to the orchard."

"Don't be so damned prickly," Eli said. "It's not like we didn't all expect this."

Zach paused on his way to the door. "You what?"

"You were best friends with one of the hottest girls in school," Jace pointed out. "We just couldn't figure out how you didn't notice that back then."

Eli clapped him on the shoulder. "So you're a slow bloomer. Better late than never, man."

Knowing any response he made would just garner more crap, Zach did the only thing he could. He flipped all of them off and headed out the door. Their good-natured laughter followed him down the stairs.

Down in the apple orchard, guests already filled the rows of white chairs bedecked with greenery and ribbons in the bride's colors. Zach knew Jace was related to more than fifty percent of those in attendance. He paused to shake some hands and have a few words on his way down to the front. Zach took the opportunity to scan the setup. He'd already gotten shots earlier in the day showcasing the white runner aisle set up between the flowering trees. Likewise, he'd documented the waiting reception in the bigger barn. All the prepwork was done. Now it was time for the main event.

Jace and Austin took their places up front. Was Jace nervous? Did you really get nervous when you knew it was right? Anybody seeing him and Tara together could see they were absolutely in sync and in love. It was a beautiful thing and one of the reasons Zach never got tired of shooting weddings. He loved seeing the hopes and dreams and new beginnings. But he'd have been lying if he didn't admit to a little bit of envy.

A whisper of movement in his periphery distracted Zach from the groom. Catching sight of Lexi moving along the outside of the bride's side, he forgot about everyone else in the area. He hadn't seen her since this morning. She'd changed for the wedding, bundling her hair into a neat, old-fashioned roll at her nape. She wore some kind of pantsuit and ballet flats she could easily move and crouch in, but it might as well have been satin and lace for how the sight of her sucker punched him in the gut.

"You were best friends with one of the hottest girls in school. We just couldn't figure out how you didn't notice that back then."

He was noticing now.

"It's time!" the wedding planner, Whitney Harrington, hissed.

Jerking his focus back to the matter at hand, Zach took his place to escort in one of Jace's grandmothers. Once family was seated, the bridesmaid processional began. Hannah Wheeler was first, followed by Avery; Jessie; Jace's sister, Livia; and concluding with Tara's baby sister, Ginny, who practically bounced with excitement all the way down the aisle. Lexi smoothly stepped in and out of the aisle, unobtrusively grabbing each shot.

When everyone stood in anticipation of the bridal march, Zach grabbed the camera he'd stashed in a potted fern before the ceremony. He wasn't looking at the back of the aisle. Instead he zeroed in on Jace, capturing his face when he saw his bride for the first time. Awe and joy and gratitude suffused his face, captured in a single tear rolling down one cheek.

Click.

Money shot.

"Dearly beloved—"

As the ceremony proper began, Zach split his attention between the pastor and Lexi. She moved like a ninja, silently slipping in and around the group clustered at the altar to document each step of the occasion. She pulled back when the vows began, swapping to a second camera with a longer lens to capture the moments without intruding.

Zach found himself watching her as his friends spoke words of promise and fidelity, and he knew that this simmer in his blood wasn't just some passing fancy. He wanted to hold Lexi. Wanted to slide his fingers into the heavy silk of her hair and lay his lips over hers. And he wanted to follow that with a whole host of other things that should have shocked him. Because this was *Lexi.* But having her come back into his life was like looking at an old photograph and seeing something he'd never noticed before. Some detail that changed the whole composition.

She looked over at him, catching his gaze. For just a beat, something passed between them. An awareness. He couldn't read her eyes at this distance, but he'd have sworn he could *feel* the same knowledge in her—that they were both grown up now.

And as she looked away, lifting her camera to catch the first kiss, he thought maybe…*maybe,* it wasn't just him.

CHAPTER 5

In the normal course of things, Lexi found shooting weddings to be a lot of work. They were long, intense days, typically around a lot of high-stress people. She knew how to wade into that and still manage to make art out of those memories, and she was good at it, as her growing list of happy clients attested. But shooting Jace and Tara's wedding was different than what she did in Austin. Because she knew him. She knew most of the people standing up there with him and his bride. And that imbued the whole thing with more meaning.

This, she realized, was the value of doing this at home, for people she cared about instead of strangers. Did Zach even realize how lucky he was to get this privilege? Did he feel this way about what he did? Catching sight of him, camera in hand as he coaxed Tara and Jace through the cake cutting on the opposite side of the table, she knew that he did. And for that moment, she envied him. She envied what he'd fallen into here, what he'd made of it, and she found herself wishing she could be a permanent part of it.

He'd let her. He'd make a place for her, as he'd made a place for her in his friend group, all those years ago. But that was taking a temporary situation and turning it into something it wasn't. She was being very careful this go-round not to do anything but accept the status quo. And the status quo was pretty damned good. Reconnecting with Zach was healing that bruise on her heart. She had friends in

Austin, but no one like him. No one like the rest of their zany crew. She already knew she wouldn't let the miles cut her off from them—from him—again when she went back. And it would be enough. It would have to be.

She was relieved when the toasts began. It meant she could get back to work, get out of her head.

The groom kicked things off, warming up the crowd with humor before turning to lace his fingers with Tara's. "It's amazing the little moments that can change your life. If I hadn't finished my take-home exam early. If I hadn't met my friends up at The Grind that day, I might not have met Tara. I can't even imagine what that life would have looked like, and I've wondered, would things have turned out the same if we'd met somewhere else? Somewhen else?"

Jace lifted his wife's hand to his lips. "I like to think we'd have ended up here no matter how we started."

Lexi took the shot, but her brain was still

turning over what he'd said long after he'd ceded the mic to others. That was the ultimate question, wasn't it? She thought back all those years to that first bonfire. If she hadn't gone, if she hadn't met Zach that night and had the chance to bond with him over photography the rest of the summer, would they have become friends? Or would they have circled in parallel groups for the rest of high school? Would he have seen her at some other time and place and thought of her as a girl instead of as a friend? Or would things have turned out exactly the same?

Unsettled, and not at all sure which version of "What if?" she preferred, she lost herself in the focus needed for the work.

After the first dance, she finally got to relax her vigilance for a moment. She wandered over to the bar set up in the corner and asked for a bottle of water. Her throat was parched. She'd been working steadily for hours and her feet were aching. She couldn't wait for the end of the night, when she'd get to go home and take a long, hot bath before falling into bed and crashing.

"Helluva day."

Still guzzling down the water, she inclined her head to Zach as he ordered a beer. He'd shed his tux jacket and rolled up his sleeves. The top edge of what she recognized as a folded tie peeked out of one of the shallow vest pockets.

He held up his drink. "To teamwork."

She tapped her bottle to his. "Seems we make a good one."

"We always did." There was an intensity in his gaze as he looked at her that made her skin come alive. She wanted his hands on her.

Don't be stupid.

She finished the water and thought about asking for another. Was it getting hotter in here?

Zach took a sip of his beer and set it on a nearby table before lifting the camera she wore up and over her head. "Watch these for a minute, would you, Joe?"

"No problem."

Lexi narrowed her eyes. "What are you doing?"

He grabbed her hand and began towing her toward the dance floor. "In most circles I believe it is referred to as dancing."

But the song playing was slow and romantic, not one of the big group line dances. Which meant they'd be dancing *together*.

"Why?" By some miracle, she managed to keep the panic out of her voice. They didn't do this. Ever.

"Because it's what you do at weddings."

"Do you regularly dance at the weddings you work?" Was his way of doing this job so much different from hers?

"Sure. I've gotten some great shots from the middle of the line dancing. And believe me, you haven't lived until you've seen the Casserole Patrol doing The Whip and Nae Nae."

The notion of Wishful's favorite trio of busybodies—who had to be in their seventies or eighties by now—taking over the dance floor distracted her for long enough that Zach managed to spin her into his arms, fitting her against him without a struggle. She'd been pressed up against him before. He was an affectionate guy. A hugger. But this was different. He was different, somehow. More... focused on her. Which was utterly ridiculous. But she was so very aware of every part of him touching every part of her as he smoothly moved them to the rhythm of the song. She wanted to sink into him and revel in the feeling of having his arms around her. Not daring to give in, she did her best impression of a fence post.

"Relax. We've covered all the important stuff. It's smooth sailing until the bouquet and garter toss and the going away shots."

"I don't know how to relax at a wedding. I'm always working." It wasn't a lie. She took her job seriously, and she couldn't imagine what her clients would think if she suddenly took to the floor.

"When was the last time you were just a guest?"

"Some of my friends from college got married in the last few years. But I shot their weddings, too. I can't actually remember the last time I was just a guest."

He studied her. "Tell me something. Do you actually do anything besides work out in Texas?"

"Of course I do." Though she was hard-pressed to remember what, right this second. Or rather, he was hard pressed. Had she realized how leanly-muscled his body was before? What did he look like beneath the starched shirt and dress pants?

"What's keeping you out there?"

She had a hard time focusing on the question. "What? My business is there."

"Your new business that you're still working to establish. You could do that somewhere else."

Lexi bristled. Was he criticizing her slow start? Did he think she was a failure? "And lose the money for breaking my lease and all the time I've put into building my reputation?"

Zach's thumb stroked over the back of her hand in a gesture he probably meant as soothing but tied her guts in knots.

"You can do your art anywhere. If you were talking about friends or how much you love it in Texas or the theoretical guy you've already said you don't have time for, that'd be something else. But you didn't say any of that."

She stiffened, more because he'd hit too close to the truth of her bare-bones existence. "What are you getting at?"

"I'm just saying, you're not so enmeshed out there that you couldn't decide to make a change." His eyes were so very intense as he looked down at her.

She forgot about the insult as she really focused in on what he was saying, her heart starting to pound. "What kind of a change?"

"Do you ever think about coming home?"

All the time since I got back. "No."

"You could, you know. Your mom would be over the moon."

Her mom. Was this really about her mother? He wasn't wrong. Lexi knew her mom missed her. But Leandra understood why she'd built her life so far away, even if they'd never overtly discussed it.

"My life isn't here, Zach."

His hand squeezed hers and there was a weight to his voice as he murmured, "It could be."

She couldn't even let herself think about this. The idea of it was too seductive, too appealing. He was too much of both, and he wasn't even aware of it. "Where is this coming from?"

"It's been so great having you back here. I didn't realize how much I missed you, and now I can't imagine you not here again."

Lexi didn't know what to say to that.

He looked down at her, into her, as they circled the floor. His eyes darkened again with that look she couldn't read, and he shifted his hold on her, drawing her closer. Her heart stuttered. Part of her wanted to relax into him. To slide her hand across his shoulder and up his nape, into his hair. But that wasn't what this was.

"What happened to us, Lex?"

You broke my heart and didn't even know it.

She swallowed. "The same thing that happens to everybody eventually. We grew up, grew apart."

"I don't want to be apart."

He didn't—couldn't—mean that how it sounded.

Except…his gaze dropped to her mouth and he was bending his head.

Ay Dios mio, is he going to kiss me?

Her pulse went slow and thick, and time turned elastic as he slowly, inexorably began to close the distance between them.

The "Cha Cha Slide" began to blare.

Lexi jolted reflexively back as the moment shattered. "I need to get back to work. Thanks for the dance."

Pulling free of his arms, she made a beeline for her camera and didn't even care if he thought she was running away.

She couldn't face him. Couldn't face what had maybe almost happened. It was better this way. She would just have gotten everything wrong again and ruined what they were managing to rebuild. He was too important to take that risk.

IN THE TWO weeks since Lexi had bolted away from him like a scalded cat, Zach had agonized, thinking about that almost kiss and wondering exactly how long it would take for things to go back to normal between them. Trying to kiss her had been an obvious mistake. She hadn't avoided him, but she hadn't been herself either. There was a tension between them, and Zach hated himself a little for putting it there. She'd opted to pretend he hadn't tried to kiss her, and as much as that sucked, he'd gone with it, keeping his hands to himself and putting all his efforts into being the friends they'd always been. As much as he regretted that she wasn't on the same page, he figured it was worth some discomfort on his part to keep her in his life. The attraction would go away eventually. He hoped.

Not that it showed any indication of waning as he sat beside her in the studio, reviewing wedding proofs on the double monitors at his desk.

"If we can, I'd like to be able to take a flash drive of previews to Jace tonight when I meet him and the guys for dinner."

"We should be able to get that far. I suppose that's a downside to two shooters at a wedding. Double the pictures to go through after the fact."

They'd both individually culled their raw files, cutting out the blurry, the poorly composed, or any other shots that didn't pass muster. There would still be paring down to the best of the best and a ton of editing to do, cleaning up and refining each one to maximum perfection. They'd already been through the ceremony and the staged shots of the wedding party and the family.

"I'd say the end results are well worth it. Between the two of us, we caught some moments I couldn't usually get on my own. Jace and Tara are going to be ecstatic."

"I certainly hope so." Lexi reached across him, clicking to add some gorgeous detail shots of Tara's dress and shoes to their folder of keepers. She didn't flinch away from him this time, and he called it a win.

"I wouldn't have thought to use this composition. I mean, I usually try to get shots of the dress before the bride puts it on, but they never turn out like this. This is art."

"It probably helps that my mother is who she is. Much as I am not a girly girl, I was raised to appreciate design. I know what goes into a dress like this, so it's natural for me to want to highlight the craftsmanship."

"It shows. You should come tonight." The

invitation was out before he could think better of it, so he barreled on, determined to reinforce the just friends thing. "It's Trivia Night at Los Pantalones. You love trivia."

"Uh, no. I'm not going to be the pink wheel."

"The pink wheel? You've never liked pink in your life." This he knew with unarguable certainty.

"It seemed as good a term as any for the token girl. No, y'all can enjoy your rituals of masculinity unencumbered. Besides, Mom and I have a date for pizza and our annual viewing of *Runaway Bride,* so I need to be getting on in a little bit to go by Speakeasy to pick up dinner."

Probably for the best.

"I think that's the last of the prep shots. Time to start on the reception." She popped out her memory card.

Zach inserted his last one. "I haven't done as much culling as I'd like from this one. I focused on getting through all the wedding party shots so I'd be able to go ahead and give them a few to share while we get to the rest."

They made their way through the cake cutting and the obligatory smashing of cake in Jace's face. Tara's expression of satisfaction made Zach snicker because he knew what was coming.

"I think the one where he streaks icing down her nose and she's laughing is my favorite of this bunch," Lexi said.

"Same."

He dragged more images into the edit folder and moved on to the shots of the speeches and various crowd reactions. When the picture of Lexi came on screen, he regretted not finishing his own cull in private. He'd caught her in an unguarded moment. A few tendrils of hair had escaped from the roll at her nape to frame her exquisite face. Her expression was soft and yearning as she looked at...well, he didn't know what. Or who. But it was how he wished she'd look at him. It was a shot that said as much about the photographer as the subject. Zach felt exposed, sitting beside her, waiting for her to say something. With half a brain he prepared to deflect her questions, to minimize what filled the high-resolution screen as nothing less than a lucky shot.

But as the silence drew out, he sensed he wasn't the only one feeling vulnerable. What did she see when she looked at this? And suddenly he had to know, even if it eroded some of the carefully rebuilt parameters of their friendship.

"What were you thinking about in that moment?"

Lexi was quiet so long, he thought maybe she wasn't going to answer.

"It was during Jace's speech, when he was talking about the little moments that change everything." Her voice was low and thick with some unnamed emotion. "I was wondering how things would have turned out if we hadn't met out at Hope Springs that summer before high school. If we'd still have ended up friends. Or…"

"Or?" he prompted.

She shrugged, eyes dropping from the screen. "Doesn't matter."

But it did matter. Zach was certain of it. "Or what, Lex?"

She still didn't look at him, and he fought the urge to reach out and cup her cheek, to tip her face toward his so he could see what was in her eyes. If he was wrong, that would tip his hand and destroy the fragile balance they'd re-established. But he couldn't stay silent, couldn't just let it go.

"If we'd have ended up friends or something else?"

Other than the subtle quickening of her breath, Lexi stayed utterly still. Like a trapped animal that thought if it didn't move, it would be safe from the threat. Zach hardly dared to breathe. He didn't want to scare her. Didn't want to be categorized as a threat. But maybe these new feelings he'd developed were a threat—to their friendship, at least. To the status quo of what they'd always been. But he'd been thinking so much about that something else, and he didn't know how to turn that off.

Please. Please just give me the slightest sign that you feel something, too.

He started to reach out, to lay a hand over hers, but the bell from out front jangled. Lexi jerked as if she'd been hit with an electric shock, her chair shooting across the room to bump against the wall. Away from him. It sliced him, that panicked retreat.

Zach supposed that was answer enough.

Quashing his disappointment, he put away the thousand questions he wanted to ask and went to be a responsible business owner.

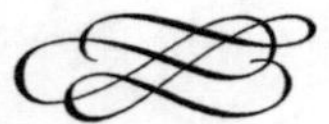

CHAPTER 6

*L*exi stayed where she was, heart hammering.

He knew. Oh *Dios,* he *knew.* Or at the very least suspected.

She shouldn't have said anything. Or she should've made something up to put him off. But she'd been so struck by the shot, by the look on her own face. Because no one but Zach could have taken that picture. And she'd wondered, for the briefest of moments, whether he felt something, too.

A braver woman would have faced him.

Would have put the question right on out there, just to let the pressure of not knowing dissipate. But once it was voiced, there was no taking it back. An axe blade hovered over the thin barrier between keeping things as they'd always been and possible disaster. If it fell, who knew where the pieces would land?

Lexi wasn't brave. Not when it came to him. So she'd said nothing and now…and now someone had given her a blessed reprieve from having to face this. Maybe she could put it off. Buy herself another day. Maybe he'd drop it, at least until she had some kind of an answer that would preserve the friendship she valued so much.

When she was certain her face wasn't on fire and she had a reasonable handle on her emotions, she followed low voices out front.

"Holy shit, dude." Zach's exclamation caused a hitch in her step.

Eli sat in one of the chairs in the reception area, a little black box open on the table between them to reveal a diamond ring winking in the light.

Lexi went brows up and mustered up some snark. "Well, this is unexpected. I hope you and Zach will be very happy together."

Eli snorted. "It's for Jessie. Now that Jace's wedding is over, I can ask her without distracting from his big day."

"Wow. That's great, man. But why didn't you just tell us all at guys' night?" Zach asked.

"Because I want to hire the two of you to shoot the proposal as it happens. She's not gonna be expecting it, and I know she'd love to have that moment immortalized."

Surprised and touched by his thoughtfulness and sentimentality, Lexi moved to join them. "I've done a few of those kinds of shoots in Texas. It's a lot of fun. There's an element of being a spy, trying to blend in with the crowd so as not to draw attention to the camera. But that'd be harder to pull off here since she knows both of us."

"Not if you're both supposed to be there anyway. I'm going to propose at the reunion."

"Awesome!" Zach exclaimed. "Of course, we'd be happy to shoot it. Have you sorted out the details yet?"

Lexi stiffened. She'd already made her position on this clear at the bonfire. Had he forgotten or did he just not think she was serious? And since when did he get the right to answer for her? She wasn't his employee. She wasn't his partner. She was, at best, a consultant, while she was in town, and they'd agreed she got right of refusal on any jobs that came her way.

The roaring in her ears blocked out the next stretch of their conversation. The next thing she knew, Eli was rising, offering his hand to Zach and getting pulled into a back-slapping hug. Lexi held her tongue, offering him a hug and congratulations herself. Her beef wasn't with him, and it could wait until he was gone.

"See you at Los Pantalones later, Zach."

"Yeah. See you there."

As the door shut, Lexi braced herself for a return to the question he'd asked before they were interrupted.

Zach turned to her, grinning. "Man, this is so awesome. Eli and Jessie engaged. Who would've called that in high school?"

She sent up a brief prayer of thanks that Eli had distracted him. But she knew it wouldn't last. "I'm happy for them, truly. But I won't be there to shoot it. I don't appreciate you speaking for me without asking."

His grin faded. "I'm sorry for not asking first, but I figured you'd want in on this. They're our friends."

"Yes, they are. But I've already said I won't be going to the reunion."

"Why? I mean, I know dances aren't your thing, really, but surely you want to be there for this."

Not my thing.

And this was the crux of the problem. As well as Zach knew her, as much as he understood her, he'd never recognized this. He'd been content to make assumptions and take her desperate agreement back then at face value. He had absolutely no idea what he was actually asking her to do, what demons he expected her to face. Oddly, that settled her a little. Whatever he knew or suspected about her feelings, it wasn't about that particular humiliation.

"I would literally rather face a firing squad than go to the class reunion prom." She meant it. Aside from the fact that she hated small-talk and had zero desire to reconnect with high school classmates other than their core group of friends—which she'd already done, thanks very much—she couldn't face the reminder of her mistake.

"Why?" His baffled expression clued her in that her reaction was totally out of proportion to what he thought was going on.

But she couldn't seem to stop herself. She felt exposed, as if any moment now, the final flimsy shield she carried would be yanked away and he'd see everything she'd fought so hard to hide. She needed to get the hell out of here, away from him, before he circled back around to try to pick up where they'd left off.

"It doesn't matter why. I'll take on almost any other shoot, but don't ask me to do that." Her voice shook, and she hated herself for that betrayal of emotion.

Zach's head kicked back at her vehmence, but he looked concerned instead of angry. "Okay. That's fine. I'll sort it out. I'm not going to push you to do something you don't want to do. I didn't mean to upset you."

He took a step toward her and she took an automatic step in retreat. If he touched her right now—well, she didn't know what she'd do. Break down? Throw herself at him? Some mortifying combination of the two?

She ignored the flash of hurt and surprise that flickered over his face. She could only handle one person's hurt at a time, and right now, hers took precedence.

"I need to go pick up the pizza."

"What? Now?"

"Yeah." Grateful her keys and wallet were in her pocket, she headed for the door. "Have fun at guys' night. I'll see you tomorrow."

For a moment, she worried he'd stop her, insist they hash this out.

But he only murmured, "See you tomorrow," as the door closed behind her.

"To the end of an era!" Leo raised his margarita. "I never thought my brother would go before me."

"Yeah, well, I haven't gotten to ask her yet," Eli muttered. "Keep your voice down."

They all cast furtive glances around, making sure none of the town's noted gossips were in hearing distance.

Reed scooped up a nacho. "What's the plan there?"

"Gonna do it at the reunion."

"Yeah?" Jace grinned. "Jess is gonna love

that. You know she loves being the center of attention."

"That I do. And she'll be happy to be dressed up all fancy and to be able to announce it to everybody fast and efficiently. I expect she'll be the belle of the metaphoric ball, showing off the ring the rest of the night. Zach and Lexi are gonna shoot the whole thing."

Zach shifted in his seat. "Actually, it will just be me. Lexi isn't coming."

Eli went brows up, setting his beer back down. "Oh, will she be back in Texas by then? She's been around so much the last few weeks, I kinda forgot she was leaving."

"Is that why you've been such a broody son of a bitch since you got here?" Leo asked.

"I am not a broody son of a bitch." Well, okay, maybe he'd been in a little bit of a funk, but he was just worried about Lexi. Worried, too, that he'd irrevocably screwed things up between them by trying to kiss her at the wedding and then forcing the issue this afternoon.

How many times would she run away from him before she just stayed gone? "And no, she won't be back in Texas then." God, he hoped not. The idea that she'd leave again before he could fix this left him feeling cold and clammy. "But she's dead serious about not going to the reunion. Like seriously upset at the idea, and I don't understand why. I mean, I know she hates dances, but this seems way outside that." Her whole response to the idea seemed entirely out of line with the situation.

"Does she actually hate dances?" Jace asked.

"She never wanted to go back in high school. Didn't like all the dressing up and fuss."

Eli sliced into his carnitas and forked up a chunk of fragrant pork. "Did she even go to prom? I don't remember that far back."

"No, she didn't." It was one of the few high school memories she hadn't featured prominently in for Zach.

"Not even with a gaggle of girls?" Eli asked.

"What gaggle of girls? She didn't have that

many girlfriends and those she did have all had dates," Zach pointed out. "Remember, she was mostly one of the guys."

"But she went to some of the other dances during high school. I remember her being part of the pack for homecoming and stuff," Reed said.

"Yeah. I don't know. Prom was different somehow. Was there some kind of thing that happened around all that that I missed?" At the time, Zach would have laid money on the fact that he knew everything there was to know about Lexi Morales. But thinking back, that was when she'd begun pulling away. He'd attributed it to excitement about the future and going off to college, but maybe there'd been more to it.

"Did anybody even ask her to the dance?" Leo asked.

Zach thought back, trying to remember. "I don't think so. Or nobody she wanted to go with. You remember how she didn't believe in things like dances. She liked to go off on all those feminist rants."

"I always kinda thought the lady protested too much about that stuff," Reed admitted.

Zach frowned. "What do you mean?"

"I mean…maybe she made a big deal about not believing in all that because the person she wanted to go with didn't ask."

"Who did she want to ask her?" Leo asked.

Zach realized he had no idea. They'd talked about everything, he'd thought. But never much about who she was interested in. "She never told me who she really wanted to go with. She asked me as a joke, and we both had a good laugh over it."

Four pairs of eyes pinned him in place against the booth.

"What?"

Leo leaned closer. "Lexi asked you to prom?"

"Yeah, just joking around."

His friends exchanged a look that clearly said, *You're a dumbass.*

"Dude, are you sure she was joking?" Reed asked.

"Of course I am. She flat out said she was."

Leo braced his elbows on the table. "Did she say that before or after you assumed it was a joke?"

Zach opened his mouth to answer, then stopped, trying to remember. She'd asked him in passing in January—part of a casual conversation about prom. He'd said yes in the same off-hand manner, assuming she was just kidding around. Months later, the week of prom, she'd brought it up again, saying they should sort out transportation and dinner plans, and he'd felt his stomach bottom out in panic because he'd asked someone else. "I thought you were joking! I'm going with Isabelle Carpenter."

She'd grinned that Lexi grin at him and punched him in the shoulder, "Of course I was joking. You know how much I hate dances. But oh my God, the look on your face. Priceless." And she'd laughed.

So had he. And that had been the end of it.

He'd gone to prom and she hadn't, and he'd never given it another thought.

But thinking back to that split second before she'd grinned, there'd been something else in her expression. He'd been so incredibly relieved when she'd said she was joking, he hadn't thought too much about it. But what if the laughter had been a lie to cover up her real feelings on the matter? What if she'd asked him to prom for real? And not as a friend, but as an actual date?

For half a second his heart leapt. Maybe she did feel the same. Maybe she did want more. Then his blood iced. "Oh God. Y'all, what if I was wrong?"

Leo sipped more margarita. "Well, I think that'd go a long way to explaining why she kinda dropped off the face of the earth after graduation. Because if she wasn't kidding, then whether you meant it or not, that was pretty cold."

Zach felt sick. "*...friends or something else?*"

He thought about how she'd backed away from him in the studio rather than facing his question. That had felt like a punch in the gut, but this… Was it possible he'd screwed up that bad? Could she have been trying to change things between them back then and he'd *laughed?* Oh hell, he hoped not. Because he didn't know how he could face the idea that his cluelessness had hurt his best friend in the whole world.

Digging out his wallet, he threw a few bills on the table and rose. "I've gotta go. I need to talk to Lexi."

CHAPTER 7

"I never get tired of this movie," Leandra sighed.

From her position curled up at the end of the sofa, Lexi managed a smile. "You never get tired of Richard Gere."

"I like his tight butt."

"Mama!"

"Well I do!" she exclaimed, in a dead-on mimic of the heroine's grandmother.

It was an old refrain, one they echoed every time they watched *Runaway Bride*.

Her mom hit the stop button as the credits rolled. "You didn't eat much pizza."

"I wasn't that hungry." She'd nibbled her way through a slice and a half, barely able to focus on the movie.

"You seem a little down, *mija*. What's going on? Did something happen with Zach?"

Not *Did you have a fight with Zach*, but *Did something happen?*

How much did her mother know or suspect about how things had gone down all those years ago? Did Lexi really want to peel the scab off that wound to tell her all of it? That sounded about as appealing as being poked in the eye with a stick.

"Nothing I want to talk about."

Leandra sighed. "Things are not so simple between you anymore, are they?"

Lexi laid her cheek against her up-drawn knees. "I don't know if things with Zach were ever really simple."

Her mother was silent for a long moment. "Come on." She reached for her crutches and shoved up from the sofa. "I want to show you something."

Relieved she wasn't going to force the issue, Lexi uncurled from the sofa and followed her down the hall, surprised when they turned into her room. At the door, Leandra paused and flipped on the light, then moved on inside so Lexi could enter.

The dress hung on the back of her closet door, out of the protective plastic, the beadwork glittering and gorgeous in the light. The sight of it squeezed her heart. In so many ways, this dress encapsulated her failed hopes. A part of her wanted to get rid of it. Donate it somewhere or send it up to Brides and Belles for them to sell so that *someone* was able to wear and enjoy it. But that seemed a betrayal. It was still gorgeous, and her mother had poured her heart and soul into making it. For her.

"I let it out for you."

Lexi blinked. "What?"

"I didn't think you were ready to give up on it. Or him."

She whipped her head around, her mouth falling open. "You knew?"

"That you asked for this dress because you wanted Zach to notice you? Yes. You've a tender heart, *mija*, and no one knows it better than me. I don't know all the details. I don't need to. It was obvious things didn't work out as you'd hoped, and that whatever happened—or didn't happen—changed everything. I know you've spent a lot of years avoiding the hurt from that."

It sounded cowardly when she said it out loud. Which was probably why Lexi had never said it.

"You've never called me out on it."

"What good would that have done? You weren't going to face him before you were ready."

Lexi snorted a humorless laugh. "I wasn't ready this time either."

"You did it anyway. And it's been good for

you—both of you—to remember what was. But I'm not blind. I've seen things changing between you and Zach since you've been back. So have you. You wouldn't be so wound up about it if you didn't. The fact is, if you can free yourself of the past, put it behind you, you'd be free to explore what *is*, right here and now. Stop holding on to what happened and what didn't happen back then, and letting that guide your life. Stop letting that hold you back from what *could* happen, if you would just take another chance."

Did she have it in her to do that? To put herself out there again? It wasn't like before. So many times these past weeks, she'd caught Zach looking at her, and she'd stepped back, telling herself it wasn't attraction, that she'd imagined it. But he'd tried to kiss her at the wedding. She hadn't imagined that.

What if she hadn't run from him then? What if she hadn't run from him and his question this afternoon? He didn't know the truth of her humiliation. And maybe he never had to know. Maybe she really could put this whole thing behind her and take this step *toward* Zach instead of away. It was what she'd wanted all along. If she could be brave, maybe things could be different this time.

Lexi wrapped her arms around her middle, anxious but a little bit hopeful, too. "I don't even know what taking that chance would look like."

Leandra cut her eyes toward the dress. "I think it looks like that. I think it looks like you going to that reunion and letting him see you as you've wanted to be seen. Go ahead, try it on. Let's see if I got it right."

Unable to resist the siren song of peau de soie, Lexi stripped down, unzipping the dress and slipping it off the hanger. She stepped into it, drawing it up and over her hips, feeling the heavy satin settle against her like water. Zipping it took a little contortion, but she managed, then she simply stared at herself in the full-length mirror. Because it fit like a glove. Exactly as it had been made to do.

She reached a hand toward her reflection. "It's perfect."

"Some of my finest work."

Lexi ran her hands softly over the skirt, where it molded to her curves. "It makes me feel like Cinderella." A very sexy, siren version, in this rich red that made her skin glow. Which was so far from how she usually felt, it was almost like stepping into another skin.

Leandra grinned. "Does that make me the fairy godmother?"

"You're certainly magic when it comes to a needle and thread. Thank you for this. Again."

"You're welcome, *mija*. But you're not Cinderella. You don't have to wait for a fairy to give you a pumpkin coach and permission to go after what you want. The power to grant your own wish has been yours all along. You only have to reach for it."

In this dress, Lexi was almost certain she could do it. In this dress, she felt brave and beautiful.

Maybe she'd go to the reunion. Maybe

she'd kiss the bejeesus out of Zach. That would get the point across without room for misinterpretation. It would change things. But her mom was right. Things had already changed between them. It was time she stopped running away from that.

The doorbell rang. Lexi glanced at the clock. Zach would still be at guys' night. Which was good. Despite the peptalk and her newfound resolve, she wasn't quite ready to face him yet. It was probably another casserole. They'd been rolling in with regularity since word got out about her mom's ankle.

"I'll get it." Lexi picked up her skirts and swept down the hallway. She loved how the dress swished around her and how the bodice wrapped her body. A little giddy at the idea of surprising this unsuspecting, casserole-bearing neighbor, she opened the door.

It wasn't a casserole.

Zach stood under the front porch light, a worried frown bowing his lips. "Hey, I…" His words trailed off to nothing as he took her in.

Lexi felt naked. She wasn't ready to face this, for him and her and this dress that symbolized everything that went wrong to be in the same place at the same time. She had no armor, no time to prepare.

But he was really *looking* at her. Her brain snapped a burst of pictures, one after another, capturing every nuance of his expression, as his mouth dropped open and his eyes traced her from head to toe and back up again, lingering at her hips and breasts. It felt like a caress, like those hands that had led her with such confidence in a dance were cupping and molding her flesh. Lexi couldn't stop the shiver of arousal that raced down her spine.

When his gaze came back to hers, it was full of unadulterated lust, and his voice was low and full of gravel. "You look stunning."

Lexi's limbs went soft and pliant. Her nipples pearled beneath her bodice and a flush of heat swept along her skin, settling low in her belly, as she let herself enjoy his very male reaction. This wasn't what she'd planned, but maybe it was Fate intervening. Why else would he have just showed up on her porch?

Before she could take that step toward him, Zach shook himself, visibly sobering. "I wanted to talk to you."

His words and that oh-so-serious expression dashed her arousal. She curled her fingers around the doorknob, as if it could anchor her. "Can't it wait? I'm tired." And that was the absolute truth. She was so, so exhausted from fighting this internal war with herself over him.

"No, I don't think it can. It's waited ten years, and I think that's more than long enough."

With creeping dread, she held tighter to the door as her mouth went dry. "What's waited ten years?"

But he was still staring at the dress. "I thought you weren't going to the reunion."

"I'm not." The words fell from her lips automatically, as if she hadn't just made a new plan. Because she had a hideous suspicion where this was headed and she didn't know how to stop it.

"Then what is this?" He waved a hand encompassing her appearance.

"Just a dress Mom let out for me. I was seeing if it fit."

"It looks absolutely made for you."

"It should. It was." As soon as the words tumbled out of her mouth, Lexi wished them back.

The lust was gone when he lifted his eyes to hers. And there it was. That potent mix of accusation, betrayal, and confusion, all wiping out the attraction that had so recently warmed her. "Why didn't you tell me?"

"Why didn't I tell you what?" But the words were an empty delay tactic. She knew what.

"That this was for prom. That when you asked me, you were serious."

She wished the floor would just open up and swallow her so they didn't have to have this conversation. She hadn't ever wanted to have this conversation. So she said nothing, just squeezed the living daylights out of the doorknob and tried not to shake.

"Why did you let me think you'd been joking?"

Lexi closed her eyes, her chest clamping so tight she could barely breathe. The secret she'd held so close, spent all this time and effort to protect, sacrificed the better part of their friendship to keep hidden, had been ripped away and laid bare. The fragile, new dream she'd just spun shattered into dust, and her nascent hope that things could be different this time died a swift death. He'd ruined all of it by finally figuring this out. Now. When it was so far beyond too late.

"Why, Lexi?"

Knowing silence couldn't be her only response, she opened her eyes and jerked her shoulders, fighting for a tone of no-big-deal and failing. "You said it first. What was I supposed to say?"

"Something along the lines of 'Hey dumb-ass, you already agreed to be my date first.'"

"And ruin Isabelle's prom?"

"Isabelle didn't matter. You did. You do."

The earnestness in his tone lit a flame in-side her, burning through her mortification to ignite temper. If he was going to push this, then by damn, she was going to finally, *finally* be honest about how much he'd hurt her.

"How can you expect me to believe that? The very idea of going on an actual date with me was so far fetched it had to be a joke to you." Saying it out loud was like wrenching open a door that had been jammed, not quite shut, for years. All the pain and humiliation that had leaked out at a trickle suddenly crashed over her in a wave, leaving her feeling exposed and raw.

Zach's face was stricken. "Lex, I—It wasn't like that. I didn't mean…"

"It doesn't matter what you intended." She was tired of this. Oh, so tired. Of the lies and the pretending, and the fighting with herself.

"On purpose or not, you hurt me." Unable to watch the pity come into his eyes, she fixed her gaze somewhere around his left ear. "And now I need you to go."

"Go? But we're not finished wi—"

"We are finished. I can't do this anymore. I'll finish editing my shots for the wedding and send them. Then I'm going back to Austin."

She started to shut the door, but he shoved his foot over the threshold, his eyes panicked. "You can't just leave like this."

"I can, and I will. I'm done. I'm just done. Go home, Zach."

Forcefully nudging his foot back, she shut the door in his face.

"Shit, dude. That's bad." Leo punctuated the statement by finishing off the beer he'd been nursing while Zach spilled out the whole, sorry tale.

"Thanks, Captain Obvious. You think I don't know that? I don't even know how to apologize for being so unbelievably clueless."

"I don't think you can. That's a whole lot of old hurt she's been living with."

Zach glared at him. "Not helping. There's a distinct possibility she's done with me. On every level. Forever." The very idea of it made him want to put his fist through a wall. Or maybe his own face. He scrubbed both hands through his hair. "I hurt her. Like really fucking hurt her."

He was never going to get her face out of his head. That twist of unvarnished grief and pain when she'd finally dropped the mask and stopped hiding. The image was burned indelibly into his brain.

"Yup." Leo's easy agreement made him want to scowl.

"I get it now. I understand what I did back then. I see how that was hurtful, and made her pull away and…basically everything that happened after because, yeah, it was shitty. I own all of that. But I don't understand why this is so fresh and raw. Why is she so upset about this *now*?"

With a head shake that clearly said I-pity-how-utterly-stupid-you are, Leo kicked his feet up on the wooden door balanced over two milk crates that served as his coffeetable. "So let's review, shall we? You were an oblivious dumbass in high school and didn't get that your best girlfriend was trying to change things. You thought it was a joke, and she went with that rather than admit the truth. Why do you think she did that?"

"Because it would have changed things. Because she was embarrassed."

"Right on both counts. So she grabs for the explanation that it was a joke to save face, pulls back, spends a fucking decade more or less avoiding you. Suddenly, she's back here, and you're picking back up with your friendship as if nothing happened."

Zack thought about the weeks she'd been back, about that initial reticence that seemed to fade as they got comfortable with each other again. Her standoffishness made sense now.

"Except this time," Leo continued, "it's you who wants to change things. You're not satisfied with the status quo, and you ultimately decide to pursue her. How did that go for you?"

He considered all those steps, big and small, he'd taken toward something more. At each and every point, she'd stepped back, emotionally and literally. "She balked."

"Why?"

Zach didn't think it was out of disinterest. "She's scared."

Leo nodded. "Yes. Why?"

"Because it would change things. Because we can't uncross that line."

"Has she said that?"

"No. But it's why I've hesitated." And it was hard not to question every move he'd made, wondering if there'd been a better way.

Leo nodded again, looking for all the

world like he was pleased a difficult student was finally getting a clue. "Right, so you pursue, she balks. And you finally work your way around to realizing your dumbassery from high school. And what do you do? You immediately go to confront her about it. No stopping to think what bringing up this obviously painful thing directly to her was going to do. No considering how bringing up this old, no doubt embarrassing event was going to impact her. All *you* could think about was getting to the bottom of the why. When all this time she's put all this effort into avoiding you, avoiding this topic because *she didn't want to talk about it.*"

"But—"

Leo's face hardened. "No, stop with the buts. There's no justifying you being a fresh dumbass. You want to know why she's acting like this all just happened? Because you embarrassed her. You dragged this thing I have no doubt she's spent *years* trying to forget out into the open, destroyed the cover story you've both been living with for a decade, and put her on the spot, expecting some kind of an explanation that demands a vulnerability from her that you, frankly, haven't earned. That's not even fresh dumbassery. That's composted dumbassery over years that has fertilized the earth for a truly bumper crop of stupid. Instead of approaching this whole thing from a place of vulnerability yourself, where you put *yourself* and what you feel out there, you cornered her about her feelings."

Defensive, Zach rose to pace. "What the hell was I supposed to do?"

"Admit you're in love with her for a start."

His knees wobbled as he rounded on his friend. "In love with her?"

"What is it you feel when you think about her going back to Austin?"

Zach's chest went tight with panic as desperation clawed up his throat. Fuck no, she couldn't go back to Austin. Not like this. Not with everything completely messed up between them. He didn't want her to go back at all. He'd been fighting that nagging sensation that he was going to lose her from the moment he'd seen her again in The Grind. Because she was the piece he hadn't known had really been missing.

"Shit."

Whatever was on his face apparently confirmed Leo's theory because he kept on rolling. "Right, so you're in love with her, and you corner her about what may be one of her greatest sources of humiliation ever. You don't just point out the white elephant, you parade that shit around in a fucking tutu, and it's everything she's been afraid of all this time because now you *know*. And everything's changed and your friendship is fucked up and it's not even because there was kissing. What is it you think she's going to do in response to all of this?"

"Run." Because that was her M.O. It had been her response to all of this from the beginning.

That was when it sank in exactly how

deeply and truly he'd screwed up with the woman he loved. The woman he'd maybe always loved but had been too stupid to see it.

Lexi was going to run and not let him anywhere near her to fix it. And she didn't have the burden of a show of friendship to maintain this time. She could and would go back to Texas and cut herself off, for good.

"Oh, God. Oh, shit. Fuck. How can I possibly fix this?" Shoving both hands into his hair, he paced a tight circle. "This is bad. This is so damned bad."

Leo stepped into his path, gripping him hard by the shoulders. "Pull yourself together, dude. Yeah, this shit is bad, but it's gonna be okay."

Zach lifted his head. "How?"

Leo grinned. "Because I have a plan. And it doesn't involve elephants."

CHAPTER 8

When Lexi had made her dramatic, mortified proclamation last night, she hadn't considered exactly how that would impact work. There were more jobs on the books than just finishing up with the wedding shots. Like it or not, she'd made a commitment to Zach that involved other people—his clients—and that meant she actually had to interact with him. Whatever her personal humiliation, she wouldn't do anything to endanger his business. That wasn't who she was. So she would put on her big girl panties and do the right thing. Maybe after another cup of coffee to fortify herself.

But the additional caffeine did nothing to stem the creeping dread as the morning ticked by and she tried to decide what to wear to armor up for seeing him. How could she even look him in the face after last night? She didn't think she could bear to see the shattered pieces of their friendship. To know that, in the end, she'd done that to them. She'd hurt him with her lashing out. In the moment, she'd wanted him to feel as raw and wounded as she had all this time. But getting it all out there, venting her spleen, hadn't been as cathartic as she'd imagined. She didn't feel free or relieved. She just felt miserable.

Her phone pinged. Grateful for any excuse to put off going into the studio, Lexi grabbed it, going still when she saw the text was from Zach. Anxiety curdled in her gut as she opened it.

Zach: **I've set up cloud access to the studio calendar. Your shoots for the week and all the relevant details can be accessed through this link.**

The next text was the calendar link.

Lexi waited for another five minutes, but he didn't say anything else.

It seemed she was off the hook for having to see him. He'd just given her the perfect way to avoid him for the rest of her stay in Wishful.

It should have been a relief. There'd be no dreaded second confrontation or awkward dancing around things she didn't want to talk about. But it was cold comfort.

He didn't want to see *her* either.

That hurt, more than she'd imagined it might. Maybe because she'd never imagined a scenario where Zach didn't want to see her. That had been the one constant in all the years they'd known each other. He'd always, always wanted to see her, even when she'd been standoffish and distant.

This was so much worse.

It felt wrong to leave things like they were. But she took the reprieve, hoping she'd manage to find some way to say…something to him once they'd both calmed down.

In the five days that followed, the opportunity never presented itself. There'd been no co-shoots scheduled. As the week rolled on, she dropped into the studio several times, thinking to rip the bandaid off. Zach was never there. Not for the newborn shoot. Not for the senior portraits. Not even when she turned in the shots for Hank and Lorna van Buren's fortieth anniversary. He was, it seemed, as determined to avoid her now as she had been since high school. Had it hurt him this much when she'd done it? When he didn't know the why of it?

She hadn't realized, until the second day passed and she'd heard nothing, that deep down she'd still believed that somehow it would all be okay. She'd let go of that hope a few hours ago and started packing. The town where hope sprang eternal was no place for the likes of her.

Lexi caught herself staring at the pile of folded clothes next to her suitcase, wondering how much time she'd lost to just standing there, doing nothing. She been doing that a lot lately.

Thank God she headed back to Austin tomorrow. Her mother was on the mend and officially off crutches, so her reason for being in Wishful was coming to an end. She'd be slinking out of town like the coward she was, without seeing the rest of her friends. She had no idea what Zach might have told them, and it hadn't seemed worth the risk of facing him again to go to the reunion tonight for the chance to say goodbye. That felt just as shitty as the rest of this situation. But surely, once she got back home, to her own studio, to her routine, she'd stop feeling this hole in her gut.

"Phone, *mija!*"

Who would call me here?

Abandoning her packing, she met her mother in the hall to take the handset. "Hello?"

"Lexi? Oh, thank God you're still here. It's Eli." He sounded rattled. Eli Hamilton was never rattled.

Tensing, she curled her fingers tighter around the receiver. "What's wrong?" A low throb of what might have been bass underscored the momentary silence.

"Zach's not coming and I don't have a photographer for the proposal."

Disbelief was quickly chased by worry. Zach should have been at the reunion. "What the hell? Why?"

"I don't know why. But I'm up shit creek here, Lexi." Eli rolled on, talking about plans for the shoot, but Lexi didn't really hear him.

This didn't sound like Zach. At all. He didn't bail on friends. She interrupted Eli's detailed recitation of what they'd set up. "Did you actually talk to him? This is not some situation where he just didn't show and might be dead in a ditch somewhere?" A myriad of scenarios ran through her mind, each one more gruesome than the last.

"I just got off the phone with him. He's fine. Well, I mean, there's been something wrong all week, and damned if I know what it is, but he's not pinned under his truck or anything. All I know is he says he's not coming, and he's on my shit list for life, and I need your help."

Letting go of the anxiety that had gripped her system at the idea that Zach was hurt or in trouble, Lexi let out a slow breath. "I don't—"

"I know. I know you don't want to come, but I'm desperate. I'm in the damned bathroom to make this call. I'm begging you, please come. Please do the shoot so we have better than crappy cell phone pictures to remember this by for the rest of our lives."

She closed her eyes, pinching the bridge of her nose, as if that would somehow stop the headache that spiked behind her eyes at the idea of doing this. If possible, she wanted to go to the reunion even less now than she did before. But Eli and Jessie were her friends. And this was probably her fault.

Lexi took a bracing breath. "Okay. I'll do it. What, exactly, is the plan?"

She was already moving to gather gear as he talked, describing positioning and the pre-arranged signal he'd set up with Zach. By the time he'd finished, she had her camera bag packed.

"Okay, I'm on my way."

"Thanks, Lexi. We owe you." The relief in Eli's voice was palpable.

"Be there as soon as I can." Tossing the cordless phone on her bed, she shouldered her bag.

Leandra appeared in the doorway. "Where are you going?"

"To the reunion, apparently."

Her mother's eyes brightened and she clapped her hands together. "Aren't you glad you didn't get rid of the dress?"

"I'm not wearing the dress." As soon as she said it, Leandra's face fell, and Lexi felt like a jerk. Wanting to soften the blow, she added, "This is work, not play. I'm not staying."

Her mother's expression turned mulish. "You'll stick out like a sore thumb if you don't. Everyone else will be dressed up."

She'd prefer to be all in black to blend into dark corners and avoid notice, but her mother made a good point. If she did catch anyone's attention, she'd have less to explain if she wore the proper attire. And at least she'd get to wear the dress once, even if it was while working. It would make her mom happy.

Dropping the bag, she headed for the closet. "How fast can you do my hair?"

ZACH WAS GOING to sweat through his tux. He tugged at his bowtie, wishing he could breathe. Nerves skittered down his spine as he kept watch on the door to the high school gym. No Lexi. Just as there'd been no Lexi for the past half hour. Despite Eli's assurances that she'd promised to come, Zach wasn't at all sure she'd show. And if she did, would she be wearing the dress? Half his plan hinged on Mama Morales refusing to let her out of the house without it. God love the woman for being on his side. He'd taken a risk calling her up and asking for her help. But Lexi's mom was, at heart, a romantic and had spent years expecting something more to happen between him and Lexi. Evidently, he was the last one to get on board. He just hoped he wasn't too late.

Staying away and giving her space this week had damn near killed him. He'd wanted to talk to her, to apologize again, to hash all this shit out until everything was right again. But rushing in and opening his mouth had gotten him into this mess, and Leo had insisted this plan was solid. If it wasn't he might just have to lie down in the driveway behind Lexi's car to keep her from leaving town and pray she didn't decide to run him over.

He fidgeted in his dress shoes, thinking

Lexi had a point about formalwear. Comfortable it was not.

All around him, people talked and laughed and danced. The gym was decked out in all the cheesetastic glory of their Fairy Tale themed prom from a decade ago. Crepe paper streamers and twinkle lights criss-crossed the room. In one corner, a Cinderella's coach picture station had been set up. The biggest difference from then and now was that the punch tonight was spiked on purpose.

He tried to remember what that night with Isabelle had been like and couldn't. It had just been another night. Not bad, not good, not memorable. She was here somewhere with her husband. They hadn't shared more than a smile and a few words of conversation.

What would it have been like if he'd brought Lexi? He should have brought her back then. He'd have remembered everything, down to the way she'd done her hair and the jokes she'd have told over dinner. He always remembered things with Lexi.

He wanted to remember tonight as the night they finally got on the same page. The night he finally kissed her. But that wasn't going to happen if she didn't show up.

Frustrated, impatient, Zach scrubbed a hand over his face.

This was a terrible idea. Why the hell had he listened to Leo? How could he put the fate of his chances with the woman he loved in the hands of someone else? He was, as he'd repeatedly been reminded, a dumbass. The whole thing was going to blow up, and Lexi was going to walk out of his life forever.

As a vise tightened around his chest, he looked back at the door. And there she was, as if conjured by his desperation.

She hesitated at the entrance to the gym, a vision in crimson. His brain snapped that mental picture and filed it away, titled *Lady In Red.* The rich, dark waves of her hair were swept up in some kind of complicated updo that left her long, lovely neck bare. Something sparkly circled her throat, dipping toward the cleavage on perfect display in the bodice of the dress. He'd seen her in it the other night and been sucker punched, but this—with the shoes and the hair and the whole package—she was so damned beautiful she stole his breath. Then he smiled as he noticed the camera bag slung over one shoulder. No pitiful clutch for his girl. It was so *Lexi*, and he ached with longing to touch her, to hold her, to see her smile again.

She definitely wasn't smiling now. In fact, she looked vaguely like she wanted to vomit, which kind of put a damper on this Cinderella at the ball moment. Okay maybe that was a bad analogy. Cinderella ran from her prince. Zach felt a clutch in his chest as he remembered Lexi had done plenty of that already.

As she so often did, she skirted the crowd, speaking to no one as she headed toward one of the tables around the perimeter to set up her camera gear. Fresh nerves beat a tattoo in his chest as he forced his feet into motion and crossed the room to greet her. It was maybe the most important thing he'd ever done in his life. He had to get it right this time.

"You look beautiful."

Lexi whirled, her hands lifting in a defensive stance. Not an excellent beginning.

"What are you doing here? Eli said you bailed."

"I didn't, but I didn't think you'd come if I asked you, and I thought you might if he did."

After a beat of hesitation, she started dismantling the camera she'd pulled out.

Panic shot through him. "Lexi, wait. Don't leave. Please. I brought you this." He thrust out the plastic box with the corsage he'd bought her, wondering if she could see it shaking.

Her gaze moved from it to him and back to it. "What is this, Zach?"

"An apology. An olive branch." A poor one judging by how her lips compressed into a thin line. Shit, he'd thought it was sweet.

She was shutting down, closing off. With a shake of her head, she turned back to her bag.

"I didn't want to come here. I don't want or need a pity date."

Damn it. "That's not what this is. I didn't mean—" Hell, he was messing this up. Again. Would he never manage to say the right thing to her?

"I don't think we have anything left to say to each other about this."

Okay, so he was going to have to play hardball. Just spit it out, however it came out, and risk botching it rather than not saying it at all. He set the box on the table and stepped closer, not touching, but making it hard for her to get past him. "Maybe you don't. But I do. You're angry and hurt, and you have every right to be. I should have realized how you felt. I should have seen that you were serious when you asked me."

Even in the poor light, he could see the flush in her cheeks and sense that she was about to run again. So he took the chance and boxed her in. "I'm sorry I was a dumbass in high school. I'm sorry for not realizing how you felt. And I'm sorry for not realizing how *I* felt until you came back into my life."

Her eyes snapped up to his, her mouth pulled into a wary frown. "What are you talking about?"

He risked moving another inch closer. "I get why you were casual about how you asked me. You were scared to death to do anything to damage our friendship. You wanted to test the waters without rocking the boat. I get all that now because it's exactly how I've felt since you came back."

The flare of guarded hope in her eyes gave him the courage to push. "You were my best friend, Lex. The person who gets me best in the world, and I've missed the hell out of you. But it's more than that. From the moment I saw you again, standing in The Grind, you just knocked me flat. I don't know what changed or why, but I haven't been able to fit you back in that best friend box I've been walking around with for years. And obviously with everything that's happened, that ship has sailed. We're never going to be what we were before. But I think we can be something else. I want us to be something else."

For long, weighted moments, she stared up at him, and Zach hardly dared to breathe. But he hoped. He hoped more than he'd ever hoped for anything before.

Lexi sucked in a shaky breath and swallowed. "And what is that?"

Lifting his hands to cup her face, he felt her tremble. "More." And at long last, he lowered his lips to hers.

ZACH WAS KISSING HER. Really kissing her, his lips a soft, insistent brush against hers, like she'd wanted all those years ago. And Lexi was too shocked to kiss him back. Too shocked to do anything but stand there as he cradled her face in his hands and changed everything. Was this really happening? Was she actually awake?

Lexi felt him tense and pull back. His eyes

searched her face, and for a moment she could only stare up at him in dazed shock. In the end, it was the raw vulnerability she saw in his face, the same one she'd felt so often around him, that galvanized her. Curling her hands in his lapels, she pulled him back, fastening her mouth to his.

And she let go. Releasing all the longing, all the want, all the need that she'd repressed and ignored for years. She kissed Zach the way she'd always wanted to kiss him. No barriers, no worries, no tentative testing of the waters. She kissed him as if she'd never get another chance.

His arms slid around her, hauling her close as he angled his head and took the kiss deeper. Her heart thundered against her chest and every inch of her crackled with nerves and joy and relief. Because she wasn't in this alone. It had taken ten years, but she'd finally, *finally* gotten her wish. He'd finally seen her as she saw him. Lexi didn't know what to do with that other than hang on to the moment, hang on to him.

It was the cheering that pulled her back. Confused, embarrassed, she realized they weren't alone, but standing in the high school gym, surrounded by most of their classmates. A few dozen feet away, she spotted Jace and Tara, Reed and Cecily, and the Hamilton twins. Eli was grinning from ear to ear and Leo offered up a wolf whistle and a fist pump.

"Oh *Dios*." Lexi ducked her head, cuddling into Zach.

Tucking her close, he rested his brow against hers. "Ignore them."

"They're making it very hard to do that."

The cheering was still ongoing.

"We can kill them later. Just stay. Stay and be my date to Reunion Prom. Let me give you tonight to make up for being an idiot. Please."

She hadn't thought he could fix it. There was no going back and changing the past. But everything about tonight was as close to a do-over as they could manage, all the way down to the reunion prom theme and the corsage he'd bought her. Not a pity date, as she'd originally thought. A new beginning.

So she smiled up at him and tried not to let the happy tears spill over. "Okay."

Zach tied the corsage to her wrist and lifted her hand to his lips.

Lexi felt a little flutter in her belly. "You matched my dress."

"I had help."

"Who?"

He offered up a sheepish smile. "Your mom."

Lexi's mouth dropped open. "You talked to my *mother* about all this?"

"I told her what you weren't ready to hear yet. That I'd messed up, I'm crazy about you, and I needed help to fix it."

She thought about her mother's insistence she couldn't leave the house without the dress. "She was in on the whole thing?"

"Yep. Turns out your mama's been shipping us for years."

"I don't even know what to think about that."

"I'm gonna go with grateful." When he wrapped an arm around her shoulders and pulled her into his side, Lexi didn't hesitate. She finally didn't have to, and it felt glorious.

"There will be squee about this. You know that, right?"

"Mama Morales can hug my neck as much as she wants. I'll be hugging hers right back."

Their friends converged.

"So, y'all good now?" Eli demanded.

Jessie popped him on the shoulder. "Hush it!"

Lexi had no idea what to say. How much had Zach told them? Then again, did it matter? They'd just been making out in front of everyone.

Leo stuck his hand out to Reed. "Called it. Pay up."

"You bet on us?" Lexi demanded.

Reed, at least, had the good grace to look sheepish. "I mean…this is a surprise to no one. We set up a pool back in high school about how long it would take y'all to get together."

Cecily sighed. "Of course you did."

Zach stiffened. "You did what?"

"Dude, it's not our fault you're an idiot," Jace insisted.

Tara slapped a hand over his mouth. "Excuse him. Apparently I can't take him out in public."

Shaking her head in amusement, Avery sidled up. "I, for one, want to know where you got that dress. It's absolutely fabulous."

"My mother made it."

"She *made* it?" Jessie asked. "Oh my Lord, that's amazing."

The girls converged, and Lexi found herself dragged into a conversation about fashion. She thanked God for her mother—not only for the dress itself, but for having educated Lexi so she could keep up with the discussion. With half an ear, she listened to the guys continue to rib Zach. And it was all so…

high school. Except better than high school had ever been.

"So when are you moving back to Wishful for good?" Jessie asked.

"When am I—oh."

Conversation around them died when she didn't have an immediate answer. How could she? Her bags were nearly packed to go home to Austin tomorrow. She and Zach hadn't discussed anything about the future. Her job, her studio, was still in Texas. How could she change her entire life to chase this new relationship with him? And yet…how could she not?

"Contrary to popular belief, we did not manage to have a complete telepathic conversation about that while I was kissing her," Zach said. "One thing at a time. Right now, I want to dance with my date. Excuse us."

He cut neatly through the group and escorted her out to the dance floor as "Save The Best For Last" began to pour out of the speakers.

Lexi's tongue seemed glued to the roof of her mouth. What could she say? How could she have forgotten all those details?

"It's okay, Lex. We don't have to figure out everything right this second. It's enough that we're here, together, dancing."

"I was supposed to go home tomorrow."

He tensed against her, then relaxed again. "Well, I'm hoping you'll give it at least a few more days. But either way, I know you've got a lot of things to think about and moving back here would be a huge decision. I'm not gonna rush you on that."

Lexi's muscles loosened. He wasn't going to push. Wasn't going to demand. This was all so new, and neither of them wanted to mess it up.

"But—"

Oh Dios.

"I do want to put it out there that I have loved working with you these past few weeks. And I know you've worked hard to establish your own studio in Austin, but I would be a hundred percent on board with bringing you on as a full partner in mine. Permanently."

Lexi stared up at him. "You'd make me a partner in the business you built?"

"We're good together. On every level. Of course, I want you here for me. But I'd have made the offer even if you'd wanted to move home and we'd still just been friends."

He'd make a place for her, as he'd done all those years ago.

Lexi's heart swelled. Oh, how she loved this man. "You make it easy."

His lips quirked into a grin. "That is the idea. Make you an offer you can't refuse."

"I don't think I could ever refuse you. So yes."

Zach blinked, the grin sliding into shock. "Really? That's it? You don't want to look over the books or talk about business plans or…"

"I want to be with you. I've seen for myself that you've built a successful business. And you were right at the wedding. I don't have much of a personal life in Texas. Everything I want is here, with you. So yeah. I accept partnership and everything it entails."

With a whoop, he scooped her off her feet and twirled. "Hot damn! I can't wait."

Wrapping her arms around his shoulders she brushed her lips to his. "Neither can I."

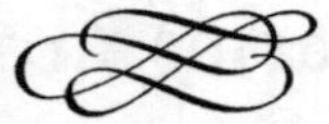

Thunder rumbled in the distance as the late August storm rolled on through town. Sheets of water fell from the sky, obscuring everything but what lay a dozen feet in front of Zach's headlights. It was a filthy night to be out, and he couldn't have been happier. He didn't even need the computer to tell him that he'd nailed the shots of the storm rolling in over Hope Springs. He'd captured quite the light show before the heavens opened up, drenching him to the skin.

Worth it. His gear was protected and he'd gotten exactly the kind of shoot he'd been hoping for. He couldn't wait to show Lexi.

He was grinning from ear to ear as he pulled up in front of the house and saw her car. It would be their house, as soon as he talked her into moving in with him. She hadn't said yes yet, but Zach knew it was only a matter of time. They'd taken everything slow on the personal front since things had moved at warp speed on the business side. But their partnership at work had continued without a hitch. Clients loved having options, and wedding season had been a comparative breeze. He'd loved every minute of having her back in Wishful.

Scooping up his bag, he made the dash to the front porch, feeling fresh water snaking down his spine beneath clothes gone clammy in the air conditioning of the truck. Shaking off like a dog, he turned the knob and stepped inside.

"Honey, I'm home!" He toed off his sopping-wet shoes and stripped off his jacket, hanging it on a peg by the door.

Strains of low jazz drifted from somewhere else in the house, and Zach smiled to himself, imagining her in the kitchen with a glass of wine as she fussed with dinner. Eager to show her his work, he grabbed the camera bag and padded barefoot into the living room.

He noticed the boxes first. A small stack of them labeled in Lexi's bold scrawl were stacked along one wall. A black-and-white photo of a graffiti arrow was taped to the front, pointing toward the kitchen. Dropping the bag unceremoniously into a chair, he followed instructions. In the kitchen, candles flickered in a neat arrangement around a champagne bucket. A bottle of bubbly nested in the ice. Leaning against the front was another black-and-white shot, this one of Lexi, big, dark eyes full of secrets and mischief. One finger pointed toward the hall. Was that significant?

Turning in that direction, he saw that a wire had been strung along the formerly empty hall wall. It had been turned into a sort of gallery, with a whole string of black-and-white shots hung by clothes pins, exactly as they would be in a dark room. Grabbing up the champagne and the waiting glasses, he followed the instructions, making his slow way down the hall.

The first shot was Lexi walking away from the camera, one shoulder bared as her shirt slid toward the floor. His heart skipped a beat before picking up to a gallop as he recognized her signature boudoir style. The next image honed in on the smooth muscle of her bare back as she eased down the straps of her bra. Zach's mouth went dry. She'd created a strip-tease in pictures. He moved on to the next picture and his toe bumped something on the floor. Looking down, he saw the black bra. In his hall floor. A little ways further up were jeans.

Holy. Shit.

A part of him wanted to rush straight into the bedroom, but she'd set up something special, and he was going to take his time appreciating her presentation. The sequence continued, each image firing his blood more than the last, until he ended at the closed bedroom door with a print of her looking over her bare shoulder with a come hither expression and a key hanging from a ring on one finger. From his bed.

Heart thundering, he hesitated outside the door, wrangling his own arousal until he thought he had some control. They hadn't crossed this line yet. He'd waited, letting her set the pace, knowing she'd let him know when she was ready.

She'd picked a hell of a way to announce it.

Zach turned the knob, opening the door.

More candles flickered in the darkness beyond, illuminating the real-life version of the picture on the door. Lexi was stunning, her hair tumbled, her cheeks flushed as she waited in the center of the bed, her pose the only thing offering any modesty.

"A-plus for presentation." His voice came out like gravel. "I want to know how you pulled this off. But later."

Her lips quirked. "You've been so patient, I wanted to say yes with a little flair."

"I'd say this is a lot of flair. Which question would this be a yes to?"

She snorted faintly. "That's not obvious?"

He knew which yes he was thinking, but he'd messed up so many times with her, he didn't want to risk it. "In my defense, all the blood left my brain somewhere around the beginning of the hallway. Maybe you should spell it out for me. In small words instead of just visual aids."

"All the yeses. To crossing this line. To moving in. To everything. I love you, Zach. I think I always have." She held out a hand to him, a real-life siren with acres of soft, golden skin. "Be with me."

She was everything he'd ever wanted, and he knew that for the rest of their lives, this image would be burned into the gallery of his brain. Yet another first in an endless line of firsts, with the woman he knew would be his last.

"Did I mention I love you, too?"

Her eyes shimmered with emotion. "I don't believe you did."

"Maybe I'd just better show you." Smile spreading slow, he set aside the champagne and shut the door.

~

WANT MORE WISHFUL?

KEEP TURNING the pages for your bonus read, a Wishful Meet Cute Romance, *Once Upon A Rescue* about a volunteer firefighter and an intrepid animal rescue racing against a Mississippi blizzard!

. . .

HAVE you blown through the entire series? Don't worry. There's more to come. In the meantime, have you checked out my spinoff series, *Wishing For A Hero?* This series is a slightly darker take on the Wishful you know and love, with a string of light romantic suspense stories that kicks off with Leo and Eli's brother Judd and his best friend Autumn.

He has one mission

Since they were children, career cop Judd Hamilton has built his life around taking care of his best friend, Autumn Buchanan. While he might once have dreamed of a different future for them, everything changed the day her father tried to kill them both. Determined to keep her safe, Judd put his feelings aside and turned his focus to protecting her, always.

She leads a double life

Nobody in their small town would ever dream that Autumn, Wishful's friendly librarian, is really successful erotic romantic suspense author, Rumor Fairchild. No one knows that the swoon-worthy hero of her series is based on her best friend, Judd. He's been fulfilling her rescue fantasies for years, and now she's ready to catapult them out of the friend zone to make her real life romance come true.

Their nightmare returns

But when the past comes full circle and Autumn's father returns to Wishful, even the power of Judd's badge isn't enough to keep her safe from the madman. If he wants the chance at a future with the one girl he's always loved, Judd may have to toss everything he's worked for aside to do the one job that matters.

GRAB your copy of *If I Didn't Care,* Wishing For A Hero #1 today!

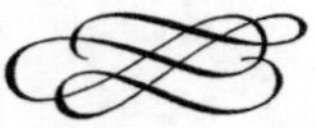

"I heard we could get up to *three inches!*"

"*I know!* I had Rick go pick up the kids from school, since they closed at eleven. I don't know why they didn't just call things off this morning and save everybody the trouble of a midday pickup."

Brooke Redding listened to the exchange in the middle of the aisle of McSweeney's Market and tried not to roll her eyes as she waited for the two women to recognize someone was trying to get by. Neither of them looked her way, apparently not realizing other people had things to do in the face of the oncoming winter storm.

"Well you know the superintendent caught all that flack for using up those snow days last year when the predictions came to nothing. They had to add days to the school calendar to make up all those standardized tests."

All around them, patrons hustled at an uncharacteristic speed, trying to beat their neighbors to the last of the toilet paper, bread, and milk in the store. Shelves were decimated, and lines snaked back from the checkouts like Black Friday at a Walmart. Everybody else was too busy stocking up on supplies to talk, as if Wishful were about to face the zombie apocalypse instead of a prospective few inches of snow.

Southerners were not known for calm in the face of anything resembling true winter weather. They simply didn't get snow in Mississippi. Snow days were a rarity and more often got used for ice storms. The first time

Brooke had ever used the sled her grandparents bought on her seventh birthday was when she'd been sixteen. She and some friends had taken it down the big hill behind the fire station, when the road had been coated in a sheet of ice and the trees had clinked together like blown glass sculptures. Turned out sledding wasn't near as much fun on ice as it had been in the snow on her grandparents' farm in West Virginia. She'd ended up with a broken wrist for her troubles.

As she didn't want a repeat performance when the roads froze later today, Brooke cleared her throat and tried for a polite smile. "Ladies, could I get by you, please?"

"Oh! Sorry." The one with the kids shot her a look of apology before beginning to push her buggy again...at the pace of an arthritic tortoise. "—Chloe started third grade this year, and I just can't *believe* how much homework they're sending home! And how are we expected to be able to teach our kids the stuff they clearly aren't getting to during the school day when they've gone and changed to some off-the-wall, non-standard form of math? What the heck is wrong with normal long-division, I'd like to know?"

Brooke's patience snapped. "Ma'am, this is neither the time or place to discuss theories of pedagogy. There is a winter storm bearing down on this town, and approximately ninety-nine point nine percent of the population has no idea how to drive under such conditions. Some of us would like to get home and off the roads before people start sliding."

As Chloe's mother stared in open-mouthed shock, her companion finally moved her buggy back and aside enough that Brooke could get by.

"Thank you." Brooke slid through, reaching across Chloe's mom's buggy for the packet of chili seasoning she needed before heading for the nearest checkout.

She wanted home and fuzzy slippers and the world's biggest vat of three meat chili. But she wasn't about to get it. As soon as she got out of here, she'd be headed straight for the shelter to see how Shelli Goff, her part-time assistant, was getting on with the evacuation. It wasn't the impending snow that had Brooke worried. It was the coinciding dip in temperatures. Forecasts were predicting lows in the upper teens for the next couple of days. Absolutely unheard of for Mississippi. The open-air kennels that made up the majority of the Wishful Animal Rescue were fine three hundred sixty days a year. But every once in a while, they had freakishly cold weather and no amount of tarps and heaters could keep the animals warm enough. That meant finding temporary foster homes for all of them until temperatures rose. If luck held, some of those temporary fosters would turn permanent placements when the hosts fell in love with their charges.

As she waited for the line to move forward, Brooke sent a text to Shelli. *How goes the search for fosters?*

Two more people had been checked out before the answer came back.

Shelli: *Not great. Nobody wants to get out in the mess.*

Brooke: *It's already started?*

Shelli: *Haven't you looked outside?*

Brooke: *I'm still stuck in line at McSweeney's.*

Craning her head, she tried to see past the crowd to the front windows overlooking the parking lot. Even from here, she could see the spitting sleet.

Shit.

It took another fifteen minutes to get through the line. As soon as she stepped outside, she flinched at the bite of ice hitting her skin. Of course they'd start with sleet instead of snow. God forbid they get the fun stuff that merited an excuse to play, then come in and eat good, hearty stews and cuddle—or other things—with a naked companion. Not that she had a companion for such activities. She'd been on a man diet for longer than she cared to admit. Didn't matter. She had way more important things to worry about than her total lack of love life. She needed a miracle to save all her animals.

Hunching into her coat, she trudged through the parking lot and headed across the street. Knowing McSweeney's would be a madhouse, she'd parked a couple blocks away in the nearly deserted downtown. The sleet got heavier as she walked, mixing with the first signs of actual snow. It stung her cheeks, clinging to her knit hat. Her hands ached with cold, and she wished she'd remembered to shove her gloves into her coat pocket this morning. Brooke was wet and half frozen by the time her little compact car came into view. Ice was already beginning to accumulate on the town green. She hustled across it, as fast as she dared, skirting by the fountain that was the town's namesake. And then she paused and went back a few paces.

This was Wishful. The town where hope sprang eternal. It was in all the brochures and on all the banners marching down Main

Street. Brooke didn't know if she believed all the hype that wishes made in the fountain—fed from nearby Hope Springs—would come true. But she figured she could use all the help she could get to keep her animals safe and in good health.

Shifting all the bags to one hand, she grabbed one of the coins she'd received as change at the market and fisted it in her freezing hand.

Please send me a miracle to save all the animals at the rescue.

It dropped with a musical *plink* into the basin.

Then, as if she'd angered the gods, the sleet seemed to double.

Great.

Shrugging off the idea of divine intervention, Brooke headed to her car and prepared herself for a long night of hard work.

"I T' S GONNA BE A M ISSISSIPPI BLIZZARD." Chester Harkin made this pronouncement with all the accumulated wisdom of his eighty-odd years.

From his position behind the register, Hayden Garrow scanned the crowded aisles of the Wishful Feed and Farm Supply. "Everybody else certainly seems to think so. We just sold out of the last of our generators, and I think we're down to two space heaters." That didn't even touch on the run they'd had on kerosene and propane since that morning. He was grateful he'd bought up one of the generators first thing and stowed it in his truck, along with a couple tanks of propane. He didn't really expect things to get that bad out at the farm, but if it did, he'd be ready.

At the other register, his boss, Abe Costello, just shook his grizzled head. "Everybody's running around, actin' a fool. They're either convinced it's gonna be the apocalypse or driving as if there's nothing at all different from a normal day."

"Well, is anything actually gonna happen?" Hayden asked.

"We're due up for a good snow or ice storm," Chester insisted. "It's been…what? Ten, twelve years since the last one? We usually get about one decent one a decade."

"Do you really think this one's gonna turn into something?" Hayden asked. "I mean, how many times over the past five years have they called for snow and we didn't get more than flurries?"

The door opened at the tail end of this, and Corbett Raines, the rookie officer of the Wishful Police Department, stepped inside. "It's definitely more than flurries. The weather's getting filthy. The rain's already turned to sleet, mixed with snow. Temps are dropping and the roads are starting to freeze. I've dealt with three accidents since this morning, from people driving like idiots."

"See?" Abe said. "Actin' a fool. They don't know how to drive in this kind of weather and don't have the good sense not to try."

Brody Jensen, a local contractor, set his purchases on the counter. "There was a guy on a job I worked a few years ago who gave the best advice I ever heard for people who have no experience driving on snow and ice. He said to imagine your grandmama sitting in the backseat, wearing a new Sunday dress, with a crockpot full of gravy on her lap, a tray full of fresh biscuits on the seat, and open jars of sweet tea on the floorboard. Everything has to get to church unscathed."

Hayden laughed and began ringing him up.

Chester considered. "You know, that's not half bad advice, actually."

"I still say people need to get on home and stay there," Abe insisted.

"From your mouth to God's ear," Corbett said. "Chief's got all hands on deck while the worst of this rolls through."

"I expect they'll have all first responders on call." A volunteer fire fighter himself, Hayden was ready and waiting in case he got called out. At just under six thousand people,

Wishful didn't have a full-time fire department—something they were hoping to change in the coming year.

Chester readjusted his stance, leaning against the counter. "Can't say I'm sorry not to be worrying over animals this go round. There's a lot I miss about having the farm, but stressing out over circumstances like this isn't part of it."

Abe shifted his attention to Hayden. "Speaking of animals, if you're gonna take that dog food delivery to the shelter, you'd best do it, or it might be a few days before the roads are clear enough to get there. This cold's coming in and sticking." He jerked his head toward the stock room in back.

"You sure you've got things covered here?" Hayden asked.

"The crazy's slowing down. And either way, we'll be out of cold-weather supplies in an hour, if not before."

"All right then. In that case, I'll load up and clock out."

"Take some care, will you? I noticed there were more damaged bags in this shipment than usual." Abe shot him a bland look, and Hayden realized he knew.

The farm supply had a standing arrangement with the Wishful Animal Rescue. Rather than taping up and selling off torn open bags of dog and cat food, they donated them. As the number of animals at the shelter had been higher than usual lately and donations from the rest of town had been down, Hayden had been rather rougher than necessary when handling the latest shipment to make sure there was sufficient food to go around.

Feigning innocence, Hayden shrugged. "Oops."

Abe just rolled his eyes. "I'm sure Brooke will appreciate your sacrifice."

Okay, yeah. It wasn't just about the animals, but about their stalwart champion with the pretty green eyes. Brooke Redding was passionate, big-hearted, and completely oblivious to Hayden's interest, same as she'd been back in junior high school. He wasn't even sure she realized they'd *gone* to junior high together. He'd been bone skinny and short back then, and his family had moved away before he got up the nerve to really talk to her. Well, he might be taller and broader these days, but some things hadn't really changed.

Saluting his boss, Hayden headed into the stock room and slipped into his winter gear, such as it was. The thermal vest and scarf didn't do much to slow down the wind and sleet slapping him in the face as soon as he opened the back door. Damn. It really was worse than he'd realized. He made quick work of backing the truck into the loading dock, then piling the bags of food into the bed, alongside the generator and propane he'd grabbed that morning. Covering the lot of it with a tarp and securing it as best he could, he climbed into the driver's seat and headed out into the storm.

~

"Avery, I need you." Brooke looked down at the list of animals she still needed to place for the next few days and rubbed at the ache starting in her temples.

"For what?" Avery Cahill's tone was full of wariness.

"I think you know what."

"Brooke, I really ca—"

"Before you say no, let me remind you it's just temporary. Until the weather warms back up. I've even got the smallest dogs picked out for you."

"It's not a matter of size."

"Then I can give you the laziest. You could keep Mulligan. He's practically a cushion with legs."

"That overweight basset hound? Good God. He's a fart factory."

He was, but that was beside the point.

"Avery, I need you to take a dog or two or I'll be forced to take drastic measures."

The line went silent with tension. "You're

calling in your favor for the Everclear incident."

"Yes. Yes I am."

"Is this *really* worth calling in that chip?"

"Two *days* of puking," Brooke reminded her.

Avery swore. "Fine. Do you have any border collies or Aussie shepherds at the moment?"

"I've got a pair of border collie-lab mixes. But they're still puppies. More than you probably want to deal with."

"You know and I know that whoever I bring home, we're going to end up keeping."

Yeah, Brooke was banking on that.

"Dillon wants dogs. He just hasn't let himself admit it yet. He's got some timeline in mind. God knows why."

"If he gets mad, blame Mother Nature and pull out the saving a life card."

"I take these puppies, we're even."

"More than," Brooke agreed. "I'll even send you home with kibble."

On a defeated sigh, Avery said, "I'm on my way."

Brooke put a check next to the names of the puppies. "I love you."

"Yeah, yeah."

"Be careful. The weather's horrific."

"See you in a bit."

Her next half dozen calls didn't go as well. While she did manage to convince her friend Cecily Campbell that her husband Reed really did need a bookstore cat at Inglenook Books, Cecily couldn't actually get to the shelter to pick one up. The answer was the same for everyone else she called. With more than twenty animals left, nobody was willing to brave the roads to come get them. The ache had turned to a full on pounding.

Across the room at the other battered desk, Shelli looked just as dejected. "Any more luck?"

"Just one. Short of going through the phonebook one-by-one, I think we've called in every favor we were owed and we're out."

The exterior door was yanked open, letting in a gust of frigid wind and a tall form with two fifty-pound bags of dog food balanced on broad shoulders. "Special delivery."

"Hayden. I can't believe you got out in this slop." Brooke rose from her desk and tried not to notice the ease with which he shrugged the heavy bags to the ground.

"With the weather turning, it was now or way late, and I didn't think you had enough food to cover everybody until then."

"You would be correct. Thank you. How bad is it?"

"Bad. The weather station's already recommending people get off the road and stay that way."

As director—dubious distinction that it was—this was her call to make. Brooke turned to Shelli. "Okay, you're done. Get home while you still can."

"But what about you? What about the rest of the animals?"

"I'll figure something out. We're not gonna both get stuck here. Go on. Scoot."

Shelli didn't need to be told twice. She grabbed up her purse. "I'm sorry I can't take any of the dogs. My landlord said after last time, if he caught me with another animal in my apartment, he's going to evict me."

"I know. Not your fault. I'll figure something out," Brooke repeated. If she said it a third time, it would come true, right?

"Good luck. Bye, Hayden."

He lifted a hand in a wave.

As Shelli scooted out the door, Brooke grabbed a bottle of aspirin from her desk drawer and dumped three into her palm. Hayden—well-used to food delivery—hauled both bags of food into the storage room. "I've got a couple more in the truck."

"More? Really?"

He flashed a grin that almost made her forget about the headache. "Somebody might have noticed you were running way low on food last time he was here and gotten careless with a box cutter when opening the last shipment."

Big, sweet, softie of a man. "You are my hero."

"I aim to please." He was out the door again in another blast of cold.

She needed it. Over the past several months, as he'd made his regular deliveries and taken the time to volunteer with the animals, Brooke had been tempted more than once to break her ban on men. Hayden Garrow was handsome, sweet, and loved dogs as much as she did. Maybe she'd have lifted her moratorium if he'd actually asked her out. But he hadn't said a word, just continued to be the human equivalent of a Labrador retriever—loyal and friendly.

The door opened again and Hayden reappeared with two more bags. "I'm gonna go ahead and tell you that your little compact car isn't gonna work on these icy roads. Can I give you a lift home after you get the dogs settled?"

Swallowing back the aspirin with the last of a Coke, she offered Hayden a wan smile. "I appreciate the offer, but I'm not going anywhere. I'm waiting on one more person to come pick up some dogs, and I'm still wracking my brain trying to come up with who else owes me a favor that I can blackmail into taking some." Her gaze sharpened on him. "Can I talk you into taking one or two of them to foster until the storm passes?"

"What about the rest of them? It's sure as hell too cold for them to stay in the outside kennels."

She liked that he jumped to the same conclusion she had. All too few people were thinking about homeless animals during weather like this. "I don't know." It was galling to admit. She was responsible for these animals and their welfare. She was supposed to know what to do. "The cats will be okay. Their play pen is inside. With a heater and some food and water out, they'll do fine for a day or two. But I can't very well shoehorn the dogs in there, for obvious reasons."

The power chose that moment to flicker and die.

"Really?" Brooke asked the Universe.

A cell phone screen let off a faint glow as Hayden switched it to flashlight mode. "Got a bigger flashlight?"

"Yes, dammit." She hunted it up and flipped it on. The brighter beam cast crazy shadows on the cinderblock walls, giving his face odd angles.

"So what's Plan B?"

Sinking back against the desk, Brooke exhaled a defeated sigh. "It's more like Plan J at this point, and I have no idea. I'm tapped out. With the power out, I can't even leave the cats inside. It's going to be too cold."

"I've got a propane generator in the truck, along with a couple of thirty gallon tanks. At half load, it should be enough to heat this core building until the city gets the actual power back on."

"Oh, thank God." Brooke exhaled a sigh of relief. "Wait, why do you have a generator in your truck?"

"Just in case. I knew the weather was gonna get bad and that we'd sell out of them at the farm supply."

"But don't you need that at your own house?"

"Maybe not. And even if the power goes out, there's a fireplace. I can make do. You need it more here."

Generous to a fault. "Do you think of everything?"

"Just about. Do you have crates for the remaining dogs?"

"Everybody but Tiny Tim." She nodded at her mastiff, who was gnawing on a Kong in the corner.

Hayden went brows up. "Tiny Tim? Really?"

She shrugged. "Well, when I got him as a puppy, he *was* tiny and had a gimpy leg. The vet figured he'd be stunted because of it but...

well, you see him." She scrubbed a hand between Tiny Tim's ears, as much to soothe herself as the dog.

"He's yours?"

"Yeah. I wasn't sure how long I'd be here, so I picked him up on my way here. I didn't plan for us both to be stuck here overnight."

His eyes narrowed in thought. "Okay, let me get the generator hooked up, and you start gathering up gear for the dogs. I've got a better idea what we can do with them."

As he slipped back into the storm, Brooke wondered if the fountain had sent her a miracle after all.

WHY IN BLUE blazes had he ever thought he could pull this off? Gritting his teeth, Hayden edged forward on the too slick road, eyes flicking up to the rearview mirror to check out the horse trailer in back. He'd learned to drive with this same horse trailer years ago—

his dad hadn't let him actually take his driving test until he could back it properly. But there hadn't been any snow or ice involved then. Keeping the thing on the road under these conditions was a whole other ballgame.

The roads were, as his grandfather was apt to say, slick as snot. Getting out like this probably wasn't his smartest move ever. But he couldn't think of a better way to transport that many animals from the shelter at once. They had one shot at this before the roads became absolutely impassable. There wasn't time for a second trip. And, okay, maybe there was a little part of him that was hoping Brooke would get stuck with him for the night. He was banking on her not being willing to leave her charges. If that meant they finally got some uninterrupted time to get to know each other better, who was he to complain? And if she wanted to express her appreciation for his saving the day with maybe a kiss for the hero...he wouldn't stop her. But that plan would only work if he could get to the rescue and back.

Up ahead of him, the rear end of a Suburban began to slowly slide toward the shoulder, the front taking a corresponding spin into the other lane.

"No no no no no." With a phantom image of his grandmother in the backseat, Hayden gently tapped the brake, slowing his approach to the Chevy.

An oncoming truck braked and did its own spin, narrowly avoiding a collision with the Suburban. Both vehicles managed to straighten up, continuing on their ways. He let out a slow hiss of breath. He could do this. As long as he kept his eyes on the road, his hands on the wheel, he could do this.

His wipers beat a frantic tattoo, swishing away the mix of sleet and snow pelting against his windshield. The sky had darkened so much, it seemed like night was encroaching already, though it was a good two hours away. His fingers and shoulders ached with strain as he poured every ounce of attention into navigating the treacherous roads. By the time the animal shelter came into view, Hayden had lost a good five years off his life. But the truck and trailer were intact.

Lights still shone from the squat, cinderblock building. Brooke's little compact sat to one side, already so coated with ice, she probably wouldn't be able to get the doors open. She came outside as he rolled carefully to a stop. Her red coat and green scarf were bright spots against the gloom of the stormy afternoon.

"What is all this?" she demanded.

"Transport. I've got a barn with room for everybody. It's nothing fancy, but there are four walls, insulation, doors that close, and I've got a forced air heater and hay we can use to line some stalls. It'll be warmer than the shelter."

She stared at him. "You're going to take everybody?"

"That's the plan. Did you have the last pickup?"

"Yeah, Avery left with her two new puppies about twenty minutes ago."

"Then let's get everybody loaded up. It'll be a cold trip, but we'll get them warm when we get there."

Brooke hesitated, her face hovering somewhere between something that might have been hope and tears. "Please don't take this the wrong way."

"What?"

She threw herself at him, hard enough to knock him back a step as her arms came around his shoulders. "I think I love you right this minute."

Hayden grinned, reflexively returning the hug. "You can be thinking about what kind of food to thank me with on the way."

The move brought her body flush with his, and though they were both decked out in winter gear, Hayden would've sworn he could feel the heat of her pressed up against him.

"I have the fixings for chili in my car." The words were muffled against his shoulder.

His stomach gave a mighty growl, reminding him that he'd been so busy at the store, he hadn't been able to eat lunch. "Now it's my turn to love you."

She lifted her head then, green eyes widening as she seemed to realize she was still holding on. Abruptly she released him. "Sorry. You're warm."

Sorry to let her go, Hayden bit back a whole host of suggestive remarks about creative ways he'd be happy to warm her up. Not the time or place for talking about shared body heat. Still, he lost some of the blood supply to his brain at the thought.

Focus.

"Dogs, then food. That's the plan."

"Dogs, then food," she repeated.

They worked in tandem, loading dogs into crates, then stacking them in the back of the truck and horse trailer. There were plenty of grumbles and howls and a few attempts at nips that Brooke shut down in a hurry. Everything was going fine until they got to the pit bull mix pacing in her kennel.

"Hey there. Hey Greta. Please tell me you are not about to have your puppies, because this is so not the time or place," Brooke murmured.

"She's pregnant?"

"Been ready to pop for a couple days now." She hunkered down, reaching out a hand to the dog.

Greta whined, nosing for pets. Brooke scrubbed her ears, then slipped on one of the leashes. "Come on sweet girl. Let's get you somewhere warmer."

"Put her in the backseat of the truck. She'll be out of the wind there…in case of whatever."

With another look of gratitude, Brooke led Greta to the truck. They made her a nest of towels and she curled up in the floorboard, still agitated.

"You can tell she's uncomfortable. I think

we're gonna have some additions to the pack tonight," Brooke said.

Hayden gently skimmed a hand over the dog's soft ears. "Fingers crossed she makes it to the barn at least."

All in all, there were fifteen dogs loaded up in the end. Tiny Tim was the last one. Hayden brought him around while Brooke hacked away at ice so she could transfer her groceries from her car to the truck. The massive dog strained against the leash, pulling Hayden off balance.

"Hold up, Tim."

The Mastiff completely ignored the order, bypassing the ramp to the trailer and leaping neatly up onto the bench seat of the truck, plopping his ass down right in the middle.

Hayden looked at the dog and shook his head. "Well, I guess Tim's calling shotgun. Get in. It's time to go."

TINY TIM LOOMED on the front seat of the truck, completely blocking her view of Hayden. Brooke was okay with that. Her massive dog might help hide her mortification.

She'd quite literally thrown herself at the man. Which, okay, might be forgivable under the circumstances because gratitude. But then she'd *held on* like some kind of moron because his body felt kind of amazing against hers. It had been so long, she'd practically forgotten what it was like to be held. And what was that whole, *Sorry. You're warm* thing about?

Lamesauce.

But seriously, Hayden Garrow was the answer to her wish. The miracle to save her dogs. Who else would willingly invite fifteen dogs onto their property for the foreseeable future? The very idea of it made her heart go gooey. When was the last time she'd gone gooey for a guy? Third grade, when Tommy Trenton gave her his last Milky Way on Halloween because he knew they were her favorite.

Maybe she was being too hard on herself with this man diet. She'd started it in the first place because of a string of exceptionally terrible dating decisions. Experience had proven she couldn't be trusted to make smart choices on that front. But Hayden was a good guy by everyone's metric. Kind, funny, loved animals, was a volunteer firefighter, highly involved in the community. And he loved chili.

Maybe she should break the moratorium and ask *him* out. After all this was over, of course. It would be awful if she asked and he shot her down, and then they were stuck together for the duration of the storm. Which, in all probability, they would be. She was under no delusion that she'd be going home tonight. Even if the road conditions hadn't been hellish, she'd have planned to stay in the barn to keep an eye on Greta.

The weather had shifted yet again, sleet giving way entirely to snow. Big, fat, fluffy flakes that would've been gorgeous to watch from inside a warm house with a fire at her back, but which made for poor visibility on the road. They proceeded at a crawl as white swirled around them.

"It's gonna be fine." Hayden's voice was calm, reassuring. "I lived up north for a while, so I know how to handle this."

"Yeah? Where about?"

"Charlotte, North Carolina. Not that it's north, exactly, but we had snow. It was a switch from Wishful."

"Wishful?" That distracted her from the agonizingly slow pace. "You lived in Wishful before?"

He chuckled. "I thought you might not remember me. I was a year ahead of you in school."

Brooke tried to remember back but couldn't seem to picture him. "How old were you when you moved?"

"Junior high. Eighth grade. My dad got a new job and off we went."

She frowned. "How do I not remember you?"

"I looked a lot different then. Short, skinny as a rail, floppy hair, glasses, braces, predictably terrible teenage skin. Believe me, I'm completely okay with the fact you can't remember that."

Brooke tried to envision him like that and failed. "But you remembered me?"

He hesitated just a beat too long before answering. "Yeah, I remember you."

What exactly did he remember? Before she could pursue that line of questioning, red taillights appeared out of the swirl of white.

"Shit!" Hayden's shout had her bracing.

Tiny Tim careened into Brooke as Hayden struggled to slow the truck without slamming on the brakes. Ahead of them, the car fishtailed, sliding neatly off the edge of the road and into the ditch. By the grace of God and Hayden's skill behind the wheel, they narrowly avoided joining it.

The truck shuddered to a halt. "You okay?"

"Yeah." She gasped it out as Tiny Tim

planted a paw into her thigh in an effort to regain his own footing. "Off me, you big oaf."

From the backseat, Greta whined.

"It's okay girl. We're okay," Brooke intoned.

"I'm gonna go check on the other car." Hayden was unbuckled and out the door before she got the mastiff out of her lap.

"Stay. *Stay!*" Brooke ordered, pointing a finger at Tiny Tim, who grumbled a protest as she slipped out into the cold.

Snow swirled around her, the cold nipping at her bare cheeks, flakes sticking to her eyelashes as she stopped to check on the dogs. They were all restless and unhappy about the cold, but otherwise fine. Satisfied they were no worse for wear, she made her way toward the car.

Hayden crouched down, arms braced on the roof as he spoke to the driver. "—don't think anything's damaged. I've got a winch on the front of the truck. I think I can pull you back on the road."

Of course he did. Because this guy was prepared for everything.

"Oh, thank you, Hayden!"

He glanced up and waved Brooke over. "I'm gonna just get you to scoot on over and let Brooke in the driver's seat for this, okay?"

Her? She slipped and slid the rest of the way over to the car, finally recognizing the big Cadillac and understanding. Delia Watson, one third of the trio known around town as the Casserole Patrol, wasn't known for her excellent driving skills.

Brooke hunched down and waved at Miss Delia and Miss Betty Monroe, her usual partner in crime. "Ladies. Where are y'all off to this very messy afternoon?"

"Oh, Brooke! Hello!" Miss Betty, also a regular volunteer dog walker at the rescue, waved back with enthusiasm. "We're headed out to Maudie Belle's place to ride out the storm."

That was a good three miles from here. Brooke exchanged a look with Hayden. Would they even make it that far if he got them back on the road?

"Let's see about getting you out of this ditch first," he said. "I'm gonna put some of these evergreen boughs in the ruts for traction."

He paused to murmur further instructions to Brooke before taking out a wicked-looking knife and hacking off a few branches from the cedar trees lining the road. Once he'd settled those to his liking, he made his way back up the incline to the road and began unhooking the trailer.

"Such a nice boy," Miss Betty cooed.

"Got a nice backside, too," Miss Delia observed.

Brooke choked back a laugh but couldn't disagree with her. "Scoot on over."

The elderly woman unbuckled and made room for Brooke. The car felt like a tank. They all three watched as Hayden readjusted the truck. Brooke really hoped he'd be able to get the trailer hooked back when this was done. A few minutes later, he disappeared behind the car, hooking the winch cable to something.

"So you're spending the storm with Hayden?" Miss Delia asked.

Brooke knew better than to look her in the eye. The Casserole Patrol loved nothing more than romantic gossip. They'd make more of this than it was. "He's volunteering to house the animals I couldn't find fosters for in his barn until the temperatures go up. We've got fifteen dogs split between the truck and the horse trailer."

"My word. Why, they must be freezing back there!" Miss Betty exclaimed.

"We've got them insulated as best as we can, and we'll get them all warmed up once we get to the farm."

"Generous of him," Miss Delia said.

"Hayden loves animals." It was the most noncommittal thing Brooke could manage.

He slapped the back of the car, then trudged back to the truck. A minute later the car lurched as the winch began to do its job.

Very gently, Brooke gave the car a little gas, carefully watching Hayden and the truck as they slowly inched toward the road.

"C'mon. C'mon." With a bump and a lurch, all four tires settled back on pavement.

The ladies cheered.

Hayden took care of unhooking the winch, and Brooke ceded the driver's seat.

"You ladies wait just a minute and we'll escort you to Maudie Bell's."

"Oh, that's not necessary, young man," Miss Delia said.

"Please, ma'am. It's no trouble. That's right near my grandparents' old place, and I'd be remiss if I didn't make sure you got there okay."

"Well, all right then. If you insist," Miss Delia conceded.

Looks out for old ladies. Check! This guy gets better by the minute.

Then Hayden met her eyes, a spark of humor lighting his, and Brooke knew she was in deep, deep trouble.

HAYDEN'S HEADLIGHTS swept over the faded red lettering spelling out "Garrow" on the mailbox at the end of his drive. Not that he could actually read it in the gloom of snow and dusk, but he knew it was there and relief flooded his system. The drive from town out to Maudie Bell Ramsey's place had been nerve wracking. A dozen times he was sure Miss Delia would slide off the road again and manage to take him and their four-legged cargo with her. But by some miracle, they'd finally arrived, seeing the two women safely to the door before driving the last mile to his own house in near whiteout conditions.

"Thank Jesus," he murmured.

"We're here?" She'd said almost nothing since they'd pulled the Cadillac out of the ditch.

"We're here."

"Oh, thank God."

Hayden parked in front of the big metal

barn. It needed a new paint job, and the landscaping around the edges was all kinds of overgrown. A project he'd meant to get to in the fall but didn't. "It's a little rough around the edges but it's solid."

"It's got walls. That's already better than what we're coming from. Let's get the dogs. I'm sure they're freezing."

As soon as he slid out of the truck, an icy wind nipped at his skin like teeth. He hurried to the barn, hauling the door open and reaching for the lights. They flickered on, and he sent up a quick prayer of thanks that there was still power. With a quick check to make sure everything was closed up tight, he went back to the truck.

Brooke was in the trailer, Tiny Tim at her heels.

"Everybody okay?" he asked.

"Cold and cranky. Let's move."

Working fast, they hauled loaded crates into the barn, setting them in a row down one side of the aisle. They saved Greta for last. As soon as she was inside, Hayden dragged the door shut, blocking out the wind and cold.

"There's still hay in the loft. I'll climb up and toss some down if you want to root around in the tack room for saddle blankets. We can set up some makeshift beds in a few of the stalls."

From the crates, an assortment of whimpers, howls, and barks let them know exactly how displeased their motley pack was.

"Hold whatcha got, pups." He paused to crank on the heat, grateful it kicked in without a fuss. It was warmer in the barn than outside just because of the insulation, but the air was still frigid. It would take a while to properly warm up. Maybe he had some extra space heaters in the house.

Brooke came out of the tack room with a pile of blankets. "It's bigger than I was expecting."

With practiced ease, Hayden tossed down several square bales of hay. "Gramps used to raise horses. Tennessee Walkers. He had twenty at one time, but that's been a long, long time ago. He sold off the last of the stock when he and Nanna went into assisted living last year."

"You don't have any interest in following in his footsteps?"

He made his way down the ladder. "I love to ride. But breeding? Nah. It takes a helluva lot of time and energy and especially money to turn a real profit there. I don't love it enough for that. I've thought about opening up for boarding, but I just haven't gotten around to it. Which works out in your favor because this whole place is empty."

Together, they made quick work of setting up a few stalls, then let the dogs loose. After a bit of roughhousing, most of them made a beeline for the makeshift beds, turning circles and ultimately flopping in a pile together to share body heat. Hayden thought they had the right idea. Not that he was about to suggest such a thing to Brooke, no matter how appealing it was to think of wrapping her in his arms.

Greta continued to pace the aisle, panting.

"Reckon we're gonna have puppies by the time this storm is over," he observed.

"Yeah." Brooke looked back at the door, worry etched across her features.

"Do you want to take her into the house?"

"I'm afraid to leave everybody else alone out here. They're behaving right now, but they aren't usually penned up together. I don't want them to do any damage to each other or your property."

"How about this." He strode down to the stall beside the tack room and opened it. "This is the vet stall. Any time we had sick or injured animals, we kept them here. There's plenty of space, it's in the middle and well-insulated. And I can get a radiant heater so that it warms up even quicker. We can set her up in here. There's even room for cots if you'd rather we sleep out here."

Her mouth opened in surprise.

"There's no way we're getting out of here again tonight." He offered a rueful smile. "You're stuck with me, I'm afraid."

"I figured we were in for the duration. No, I just…you don't have to stay out here with me."

Was she saying that because she didn't want to spend time with him or because she felt bad about sentencing him to a long, cold night when the house was twenty-five yards away?

Hayden shrugged. "Won't be the first night I've spent in this barn. Let me go grab some more supplies. If you want to bring in your groceries, there's a little fridge and a hot plate in the tack room. I'll grab some kitchen stuff and you can get started on that thank you chili, like you promised."

Brooke stared at him, brows knit.

Uncomfortable with the scrutiny, he rocked back on his heels. "What?"

"You were a Boy Scout, weren't you?" Her tone held a tinge of accusation.

"Eagle Scout. Why?"

"Because you're apparently prepared for everything." At last, she smiled and it hit him right in the solar plexus, warming him like a shot of whiskey.

No, he hadn't been prepared for everything. He hadn't been prepared for her. Needing the distance to get himself under control, he said, "I'll be back," and stepped out into the storm.

SHE WAS SPENDING the night with Hayden Garrow.

Okay, so it was in a barn with fifteen dogs, but still. Brooke couldn't read him. Couldn't tell if this was just his usual friendliness or something else. She was starting to *really* wish for the something else.

She made quick work of bringing in the groceries and stowing them in the…well, the facilities in the tack room weren't even big enough to merit the designation of kitch-enette. But she did find the hot plate and a few other kitchen basics, including a sizable crock pot. It wasn't much, but she could probably manage chili with all that. Plugging in the slow cooker, she flipped it on high to start warming and turned to browning the first batch of meat on the hot plate. The scent of chorizo began to waft out of the tack room and on into the barn, drawing several of the dogs like the pied piper's song, including her own gentle giant.

"Not for you. Shoo." She waved them out of the tack room and shut the door.

A few minutes later, she caught the murmur of Hayden's voice, presumably talking to the dogs. Then he was gone again to get another load of stuff. Once she got the chili in the crock pot, she'd go help with what-ever was left.

The tack room door opened as she scraped the last of the meat into the crock.

"Something smells amazing." Hayden

peered over her shoulder into the crock pot. "Is that bacon?"

He wasn't touching her, but Brooke could feel the heat of him along her back. Which was ridiculous. It wasn't as if he was a human furnace. Still, awareness raised the hair on her arms as she answered. "Beef, chorizo, and bacon, yeah. It's the basis for my three meat chili."

He tugged off his knit cap and clutched it over his heart. "Marry me. You are clearly the perfect woman."

Okay, maybe he wasn't just being friendly. Brooke could work with that. She pivoted where she stood and shot him a flirty smile. "Well, you did save all my dogs."

"Least I could do." He didn't step back, didn't move any closer. He just stood there, inside her personal space bubble, searching her face.

Brooke cleared her throat. "I just need to get the tomatoes, sauce, spices, and beer in. I couldn't find a—"

He produced a can opener from a pocket.

"Boy Scout," she said again. Her fingers brushed his as she took it and another frisson of awareness zapped up her arm.

"Chili lover," he corrected.

Brooke's fingers clenched around the can opener, as if it might ground her. "Can I help you carry anything else from the house?"

"Got it all already. Finish up here, I'll get everything sorted." He left her to it.

As soon as he'd shut the tack room door behind him, she let out a slow exhale and turned back to the crock pot.

Seriously, how had they been working together off and on for months at the shelter and she never noticed this attraction before? She'd thought he was cute and definitely she'd started noticing his muscles. But they'd just been friends. Not even hang out friends, just…we-work-together-at-the-shelter-and-he's-a-regular-volunteer kind of friends. He'd had a sort of…maybe not hands-off vibe, but she'd never sensed any kind of a want from him before. Or maybe it was that she didn't consider herself available before, so she hadn't been tuned in to that. Or maybe she was crazy to think that there might be a little prospective snow-bound romance happening here.

By the time she came out of the tack room, he'd set up two cots in the vet stall, complete with thermal sleeping bags and pillows. Another heater had been plugged in and was already warming the space. Greta was finally settled on a nest of towels in the corner. And in the aisle, he'd laid out a pile of quilts, several deep over the concrete floor. A basket anchored one corner, next to a massive urn of what she was optimistic enough to hope was coffee. And in his hands was a pack of Oreos he was trying to keep out of the maw of Tiny Tim. The other dogs had apparently been shut into their stalls.

"Are we having a picnic?" she asked.

"I mean, if we're gonna be out here anyway..." The tips of Hayden's ears pinked. He lifted the Oreos. "I figured dinner would be a while and you might be hungry."

The gesture was sweet and thoughtful, just the latest in a long line of sweet and thoughtful. Stuff she'd chalked up to him just being a nice guy. But maybe there was more to it than that. God knew, she could really use a nice guy.

"Thank you. I'm starved."

They each grabbed a saddle from the tack room to use as a backrest and settled in on opposite sides of the package of cookies. He'd brought half and half and sugar in the basket, along with an assortment of other snacks he'd clearly foraged from his own kitchen. Chips and salsa, cheese and crackers. Between all that and the chili, they certainly wouldn't starve.

"So tell me, how did you get into the rescue business?"

Settling back against her saddle, clutching the deliciously warm mug between her palms, Brook admitted, "I'm a vet school drop out."

"Really? That surprises me."

"Yeah, I went to Mississippi State. I made it through the second year but I just…couldn't handle it. I love animals, and I couldn't cope with having to deal with their pain every day. The idea of having to put an animal down, even as a mercy, just killed me. So I quit. I ended up switching over to get a bachelor's degree in veterinary technology so that I had *something* while I figured out what to do with my life."

As she told her story, Tiny Tim gave an insulted grumble and flopped down on the blanket, ass end toward her to let her know what he thought of her failure to share the cookies. Well knowing her role here, she scratched at the base of his tail. "I kind of fell into the job here when my predecessor broke her leg. Massive spiral fracture. She ended up with a rod and everything. I'd been volunteering here all through college, over breaks and during the summers, so I knew the ropes and the structure. It made sense at the time, and it was just supposed to be a temporary takeover while she recovered. That was three years ago."

"You run the whole thing by yourself?"

"Well, there's me as the only full-time employee. Shelli's my part-time assistant, and there are, as you know, scads of volunteers."

He blew on his coffee. "Even with volunteers, that's a lot of work for one and a half people. There are always more animals that need help and never enough money. That's the story of rescues and shelters everywhere, right?"

"I keep the whole thing afloat with donations and grants and a lot of hair pulling and sleepless nights. My parents keep waiting for me to get a real job, but they don't understand this *is* a real job. It's just not the job they wanted for me." They'd expected something normal, in an office. The kind of soul-crushing job they'd both worked their whole adult lives. "There's absolutely nothing better than seeing an animal find a new forever home. Sure as heck beats corporate culture."

"You love it."

"Yeah, yeah I do. There's stress, of course. I've been wracking my brain for months trying to figure out how to raise enough money for a new facility or even some kind of renovation to enclose the outdoor kennels. They were calling for a stiff winter months ago. I just…didn't come up with anything. If you hadn't come along, I don't know what I'd have done." She swiped up another Oreo and dunked it in her coffee. "What about you? You said you moved away from Wishful in junior high. Obviously you came back. Why was that?"

"When I finished college, I was at loose ends, not quite sure what I wanted to do. My grandparents were starting to slow down and needed some help, so I came at first to help them out with the farm and do all the stuff my granddad was getting too arthritic to do. When it came time for them to move into assisted living, the only reason Gramps agreed was because I said I'd stay on at the farm. So, here I am."

What a sweetheart.

Brooke didn't realize she'd spoken aloud until Hayden's cheeks flushed to match his ears.

"It's what you do for family. Besides, Wishful was always home. Plus, it's not exactly a hardship these days to be given a place to live that's free and clear."

Thinking of the money she spent every month in rent, she angled her head in concession of the point. "You are not wrong."

The temperature had climbed into a more comfortable range, still chilly, but not the frigid bite of outside. The coffee had helped tremendously, thawing her from the inside out. The savory, spicy scent of chili filled the space, and with the sound of snoring dogs, she could almost pretend they were on some kind of indoor camp out. It was cozy and surprisingly comfortable. Far more than she'd been expecting.

Hayden rolled to his feet, offering a hand. "C'mon. Let's see what the damage is."

He tugged her up, his hand lingering on hers for a moment before he stepped off the blanket and moved toward one of the windows in the front. Almost cheek to cheek, they peered out. Beyond the glass, the snow had slowed down to less blizzard-like conditions, but there were clearly several inches of accumulation already.

"We haven't had snow like this in my lifetime," Brooke murmured.

"I'm sorry you got stuck."

She turned her head to look at him and decided to take the leap. "I'm not."

FEELING the weight of her gaze, Hayden turned his head to meet those pretty, evergreen eyes. "You're not?"

Brooke shook her head, her gaze dropping to his mouth before slowly coming back up to his eyes. As a sign, that was a pretty damned hard one to misread. He searched her face anyway, waiting for the spell to break or awkwardness to descend. When she didn't move, only waited, he decided he'd never been so grateful for snow in his life.

"Me either," he whispered.

The air went thick with anticipation.

With the same level of caution he'd use to approach a wary dog, he closed the distance between them, keeping his eyes on hers. A breath away from her lips, he paused, letting the tension build and roll along his skin like a wave. Brooke lifted a hand to his chest. He could barely feel the press of it through the puffy vest, but he certainly noticed when her fingers gripped the fabric and yanked him forward that final inch. He was smiling when her lips closed over his.

Her mouth was warm, a contrast to the pulse of cold from the window beside them. On a sigh, she swayed into him, turning the bare brush of lips into something deeper. Needing no further invitation, Hayden wrapped an arm around her, drawing her in and lifting a hand to her nape to finger the edge of her short cap of hair. The silk of it teased his fingers. Her hands slid up his chest, fumbling until she found the zipper to his thermal vest. She lowered it, the sound penetrating the roaring in his ears to kick his pulse into high gear. Did she feel it pounding when she slid her arms around his waist beneath the vest, drawing them chest to chest, warmth to warmth? Her own pulse beat a steady thud against his palm. He stroked a thumb over that point of heat until he felt his control and good intentions begin to fray. Only then did he ease back.

Brooke dropped back to her feet and ran her tongue over her lips. The gesture had half the blood draining from his head.

"Sweet," she murmured.

"Huh?"

"You taste like Oreos."

That had him chuckling. "Double dessert before dinner. That works for me."

One corner of her mouth lifted in a lopsided smile. "I've been thinking about that all afternoon."

"I've been thinking about it since junior high."

Surprise had her tipping her head back. "What?"

Damn. He hadn't meant to say that out loud. Well, he was in it now. "I had a terrible crush on you back then."

"Really?"

"The girl who had her own daily bake sale to fund her cause of the month. Always something animal-related."

Brooke blinked. "Wow. That makes me feel terrible I don't remember you."

"Believe me, it's better that way. You were out of my league back then."

"It was junior high in a small town. There was no league."

"Keep telling yourself that." Because she

tempted him to fall into another kiss and well beyond, Hayden made himself take a step back. He wanted more than a quick roll in the proverbial—or, given their location, quite literal—hay with Brooke. "The chili will take a while longer, right?"

"It's one of those things that gets better the longer it cooks."

He jerked his head toward the door. "The snow's slowed down. There's no telling how long it will actually last in the morning. You wanna go play?"

Her grin spread wide. "Hell yeah."

They checked on the dogs one last time and made a run to the house for some extra layers, but fifteen minutes later, they began scooping and packing snow.

"With all this, we'll be able to make a snow village!" Brooke declared.

"It'll be a damn sight better than the pitiful snowman I managed my last winter here. He was only two feet tall."

"Two feet's good for a Mississippi snowman. Most of mine were only a foot. I have a pictorial chronicle of all the Bobs."

"Bobs?"

Her self-deprecatory laugh was dampened by the snow. "Every snowman I have ever built has been named Bob. I have no idea why. It's just a thing I started when I was a kid."

"And what number Bob are we on today?" Hayden asked.

She paused in the midst of enlarging the base. "I think this would be Bob the Tenth."

"That's a lot of Bobs for a Southern gal."

"My grandparents live in West Virginia. We go up there for Christmas every other year, so I usually get the chance to play in real snow. When I was in first grade, I made a snowball and put it in a big mason jar to bring back for show and tell since nobody really knew what snow looked like down here."

He laughed. "And did your prize survive the trip home?"

She feigned a devastated expression.

"Sadly, no. I lost out on cementing my coolness for yet another year."

"You're still cool in my book." Scooping up snow on the fly, Hayden balled and flung it in her direction. The snowball went splat against her red coat, eliciting a squeak of surprise.

"Snowman building is the neutral zone!"

"All's fair in snow and war," he declared.

Instantly, she bent to retaliate. A face full of snow was a frigid reminder that she'd played softball as a kid. She still had a hell of an arm. Her giggle lit the air as he wiped snow from his face.

"Okay then. It's on."

They played like children, pelting each other with snowballs and dodging in and around the barnyard until he finally snagged her when she shoved a snowball straight down the back of his shirt.

"You're going to pay for that!" He dragged her down with him, rolling until she was pressed beneath him, breath heaving, cheeks rosy, and eyes snapping with mischief. There was nothing to do but kiss her.

Her response was immediate. She arched up to him, wrapping her arms around his shoulders and opening her mouth beneath his for a string of hot, playful kisses that had him wishing for a bed and far fewer layers. Brooke shared the sentiment, her frozen fingers snaking beneath his shirt to splay against his back.

Hayden let out a pitifully unmanly yelp at the touch. "Holy crap, woman, your hands are freezing."

"That's what happens when you make out in a snowbank."

Laughing, he dropped his brow to hers. "How about we take this inside where it's warmer?"

"I support this plan."

With one, last, fleeting kiss, Hayden tugged her up, only now noticing his wet jeans and hers. They'd need fresh clothes and towels. At the risk of breaking the mood, he stopped at the door. "In the name of avoiding hypothermia, I'm gonna run into the house to grab some dry clothes for us both, okay?"

"I'll check on the dogs." She skimmed a hand over his cheek. "Hurry back."

"Yes, ma'am."

REVVED UP WITH AROUSAL, Brooke barely noticed the cold. She hadn't quite decided how far this was going to go, but definitely further. She wanted to get her hands on him, wanted his hands on her. Wanted more kissing. Definitely more kissing. She'd forgotten how much she loved kissing, and Hayden was particularly good at it.

Inside, assorted canines offered greetings. She went stall to stall, checking on the group. There'd been no fights, no fussing. The lot of them mostly just seemed happy to be out of the worst of the cold. And then she reached the vet stall. Greta was in active labor.

The priority shift was instant. Brooke slipped inside, moving slowly lest the dog decide to snap. But Greta had bigger things on her mind. Brooke was still kneeling in the straw, checking Greta over when Hayden came back.

"She doing okay?"

"Her labor's starting. She's doing fine, so far." Brooke rose to her feet and joined him at the door to the stall.

His eyes searched her face. "You worried?"

"No. Just…cautious. Mostly dogs don't need our help, but there's that whole fact that we can't *get* to any if she does."

"I heard somebody around here was a vet tech and actually knows stuff."

She shot him a look at the bland tone. "Ha ha. Yeah, I can handle minor stuff. But whatever happens is going to happen, so I'll leave her to it."

"You should get out of those wet clothes." There was nothing salacious in his tone as he offered up a pile of towels and clothes.

With a rueful smile, she took the pile. "Not the context where I was hoping to hear those words."

A flash of heat crossed his face. "Not right now isn't the same as never."

It fascinated her how he could bank the desire and shift priorities so quickly. Always putting others first. She liked that about him. It set him apart from the long string of duds that had inspired the man diet in the first place and made Hayden, by her estimation, the perfect guy to break it with.

"No, I suppose not." She took the pile. "We should work on a collective potty break for the pack before we bother putting on dry clothes."

"Fair point. If there's more snow coming, now's as good a time as any to do it."

"*Is* there more snow coming?"

"No idea. Would you mind if there was?"

"I can't think of anybody I'd rather be snowbound with."

"Back atcha, Blondie."

It took almost half an hour to let everybody out. Without a proper fenced yard, they couldn't risk letting anybody but Tim off leash. All the dogs wanted to sniff, several wanted to play, and Mulligan freaked out about the snow, which was up to his belly. By the time everybody was settled again, she was feeling the cold all the way in her bones and looking forward to chili and dry clothes.

Settling the dogs with chew bones, Brooke disappeared into the tack room to change. He'd brought her some of his own clothes—a henley and flannel shirt, some sweatpants. Unable to resist, she buried her nose in the soft flannel and sniffed. The shirt smelled like him, a comforting mix of sweetgrass and cedar that was probably as much detergent as man. The scent immediately calmed her.

She'd been shockingly calm in general this afternoon, since he'd strode into the rescue with the plan she'd so desperately needed. She was always less stressed when Hayden was around. He had a habit of wading in and helping out, knowing exactly what was needed. She'd seen it before today but hadn't had occasion to really think about how much his easy assistance was truly worth. For someone like her, used to handling things all on her own, that was more than a little appealing. As if she needed more reasons to like him.

When she emerged from the tack room, she found he'd changed himself into another variation of his winter uniform of henley and flannel. His wet clothes were draped on one of the stalls to dry. She followed suit, wondering if her own clothes would be wearable by morning. While the barn had warmed considerably, she bet it was hovering right around sixty degrees. Not exactly conducive to air-drying laundry.

"The chili's ready," she announced.

"Perfect. I'm starved." But it wasn't the empty belly kind of hungry she saw on his face.

"Is everything we say going to sound suggestive now?"

"Probably. I figure it's a symptom of make-outus interruptus. That a problem?"

"No. Just checking to see if it was just me."

"Definitely not just you."

"Good to know." It was a long night ahead. Perhaps there'd be opportunity to pick back up where they'd left off. The idea of it had her skin flushing.

"I am legitimately looking forward to that chili."

"I should hope so since you proposed marriage. That's a serious offer to be making without tasting it first."

"Obviously I need to rectify the oversight."

They grinned at each other.

In the tack room, she dragged out the sour cream and cheese, opening the tortilla chips and setting up a line of fixings on the battered old desk. They dished up the food in a couple of hand-thrown pottery bowls he'd brought from the house and ate the first serving standing around the crock pot. For the second, they relocated to the picnic blanket, where he pulled something from his pocket.

"How do you feel about cards?"

She went brows up. "Poker?" In a game of strip poker, she'd be the definite loser, winding up down to her underwear before he even lost his socks. Under some circumstances that might be okay, but it was way the hell too cold for that tonight.

His grin turned a little bashful. "Gin rummy."

Delighted with him, she laughed. "You, Hayden Garrow, are turning out to be quite the surprise."

He shuffled the cards and bridged them with all the expertise of a Vegas pit boss. "My Nanna was a bit of a card shark. She taught me to take no prisoners."

"Noted. So what are the stakes?"

"Stakes?"

"What are we playing for? Just bragging rights or something more interesting?"

"I'm game for more interesting. How about kisses?"

"That seems rather mutually beneficial for stakes," she observed, feeling a tightening low in her gut.

"Does that offend your competitive spirit?" he teased.

"Competition is overrated."

Grinning, he began to deal.

MORNING CAME with a warm woman in his arms, her face pressed into the bared skin of his throat, their legs tangled beneath the heavy sleeping bag. Hayden decided it was a pretty amazing way to start the day, even if they were both wearing multiple layers apiece. Then the barking started. A yip here. A whine there. Within moments there was a cacophony of canine demands.

Brooke groaned and snuggled closer. "Time s'it?"

"Not sure. Daylight. Breakfast according to the starving masses."

She stretched on another moan, her body rubbing enticingly against his and the blood drained out of Hayden's head. Under the guise of stretching himself, he eased his hips back.

Blissfully unaware of his state, Brooke sat up, wrapping her arms around her middle. "God, it's so cold."

Her hair stood on end in charming disarray, and her cheeks were flushed and rosy with sleep. Utterly gorgeous.

Unable to resist the urge, Hayden hooked a hand around her nape and drew her mouth to his. She jolted once before melting into him, her hands fisting in his shirt. Knowing they had work to do, he kept the kiss light and easy, just enough to appease the craving for closeness.

"Good morning," he murmured.

Brooke blinked at him, green eyes hazy with sleep and desire. "That's a helluva good morning."

Hayden grinned. "I'll do you one better. Go check on the puppies. I'll start the potty routine and once we're done, I'll make pancakes."

"Throw in fresh coffee and you will have my undying gratitude."

"I thought I already had your undying gratitude," he teased.

"Fine. I'll give you my chili recipe."

"Deal." As the dogs hadn't slowed down their complaining, he hollered, "I'm coming! I'm coming." He shoved his feet into boots and shrugged on his coat.

He and the first three dogs came out of the barn into a winter wonderland. The snow had continued through most of the night, filling in a lot of the tracks from their snowball fight. There was certainly enough to complete the abandoned snowman this morning. While the dogs sniffed and did their business, he checked his phone, reading the backlog of texts that had come in since last night.

Brooke joined him as he brought in the second group of dogs. "Puppies are doing just fine. All six came through the night and mama's doing well."

"Good to hear. Looks like we ended up with about six inches, all told. The roads aren't clear yet, but the Department of Public Works has already started clearing in town."

"How do you know all that?"

"Fire Department group text. We've been doing running updates since the storm started yesterday. Thankfully there weren't any major emergencies while the roads were shut down."

"Thank God for small miracles."

As soon as the dogs were settled again, they retreated to the house. Belatedly, he wondered if he should've made an effort to clean up. But Brooke didn't comment on the evidence of his bachelorhood scattered around the living room and kitchen.

"Oh my God, heat! This feels glorious!"

"If you want to throw your clothes into the dryer to warm them up before you change again, you're welcome to. I'm gonna get started on breakfast."

While she was in the laundry room, he made a quick pass through the house to make sure he hadn't left underwear or anything else mortifying lying around. He scooped up empty glasses and the takeout containers piled on the coffee table. That would have to do.

Brooke had started the coffee herself. He liked that she was comfortable enough to make herself at home and wondered if that was just how she was or if it had something to do with the fact that she was still wearing his clothes. It was a curious sort of intimacy, along with a host of others they'd crossed since yesterday because of their snowbound state. Would she backpedal once things got back to normal? He didn't want that. He wanted this to be the start of something real, and he had some ideas on how to make that so.

"Did your magic group text happen to say what the weather report was?"

"The cold is here for a couple more days, though the snow is finished. We should be able to get out to go check on the cats by this afternoon."

Her shoulders relaxed a little at that. "I guess you're stuck with us for a little while longer."

"I've got no problems with that. While we're out, we'll swing by your place to pick up some more clothes. Not that I have a problem seeing you in mine."

Her answering smile came with a blush. "I really can't thank you enough for all your help with this. I don't know what I'd have done if you hadn't rescued us."

Hayden saluted. "I live to serve." Turning away, he began to mix up the pancake batter. "Have you given any thought to what you're going to do about the rest of winter? We probably won't get snow again, but this isn't likely to be the last of the cold."

"You're right. It's not. And I really don't know. I've got some grants submitted for funding that I'm waiting to hear on. But that likely won't come through until spring. If we weren't already at capacity, I could probably jury rig something that would get us through, but we're busting at the seams. With six new mouths to feed as of last night."

"I had an idea about that, actually."

"I'm all ears."

"I think you should move the shelter out here."

Brooke paused, the coffee halfway to her lips. "I'm sorry?"

"The barn is much bigger than the facility you've got and could be adapted to house kennels and such. It's not being used for livestock and isn't going to be." He added a cheeky grin. "Plus, it means I'd have an excuse to see you more often."

Her expression softened and she pushed up from the chair, padding across the room in sock feet to slip her arms around him. "Did you need an excuse?"

He tucked her closer. "You tell me."

"Heroes are always welcome." She rose to her toes and brushed her lips over his in a quiet kiss, full of affection and gratitude. "I appreciate the thought and your willingness to just offer up your space, but I don't think that's the answer. At least, not on any kind of permanent basis."

"Why?"

"You said yourself you'd been thinking about opening up the barn for boarding. You might need that income. Beyond that, it would put the rescue very much in your space. There's the noise from the animals, not to mention, serious implications for the future salability of the property."

"We're not selling the farm."

"Maybe you won't. But if it came up, that would be a problem. Plus, it's a fair bit out from town and there's a lot of legal implications with permits and stuff." She softened her refusal with a wry smile. "Besides, what happens if you get sick of me?"

Hayden didn't see that happening, but he wasn't going to force the issue. "Fine. But at least consider it as a temporary solution this season."

"Now that I will absolutely do. Thank you."

"You can thank me by pouring me a cup of that coffee while I finish these pancakes."

"You got it."

As she turned away, rummaging in the cabinet for a mug, Hayden shot off a quick text. Let it not be said that he didn't think on his feet.

AFTER BREAKFAST, Brooke had a shower—a glorious, steaming shower that thawed her out all the way for the first time since yesterday—and finally felt ready to face the rest of the day. Once the roads were cleared, she and Hayden piled into his truck to go check on all the animals still at the rescue. He was quiet on the drive. Brooke glanced over at him from beneath her lashes, trying to gauge his mood. She felt bad for shooting down his idea, but generous though it was, it wasn't practical. And if this attraction ended up being the product of forced proximity rather than something real, she didn't want the strain on either of them of working where he lived.

Brooke deflated, her pleasure in the morning waning. She didn't want this to be just a fluke of shared space and body heat. Hayden was sweet and funny and interesting. He was a good man, which already put him leaps and bounds ahead of the last guys she'd dated. She wanted the chance to get to know him better. Wanted to pursue the chemistry between them to see where it led. She wanted to prove to herself that her judgment wasn't permanently flawed.

The driveway of the shelter hadn't been cleared. Hayden's truck bumped and slid down the road, coming to a stop beside her car, which was coated in a fluffy layer of white. Nothing interrupted the winter quiet but their footsteps as they trudged through the snow toward the entrance.

"Generator's off," Hayden noted. "Either it ran out of propane or the power's back on."

"Fingers crossed for the latter." She unlocked the door and stepped inside. The interior was blessedly warm. Lights flickered on when she flipped the switch. "Hooray for power."

"I'll go unhook the generator and load it up while you check on everything."

Dumping her purse, she opened the door to the back. A chorus of opinionated meows greeted her as she stepped inside.

"Hey, y'all. Who's hungry?"

Relieved the cats had survived the night, no wiser to the severe winter weather, she lost herself in the routine of cleaning cages, dishing out food and water and offering up a few brief cuddles to those felines who were so inclined. She kept expecting Hayden to walk in. When he hadn't materialized by the time she finished, she went in search of him.

He was in the kennels, pacing around the outside edges.

Shoving her hands into her coat pockets, she circled around to join him. "What are you doing?"

"Thinking. You've got these aluminum carport covers over all the kennels. I've seen people make barns out of these. I think we could use the same concept to close this in and insulate it."

"Really?" The idea of it intrigued her.

"Come on, I'll show you."

Taking her hand in his, he walked her through it, pointing out the steps to how the entire facility could be enclosed and weatherproofed. It would cost money—everything did—but what he proposed would cost a lot less than building something from scratch.

Fresh stirrings of hope had her turning toward him. "This is a great idea. Certainly more affordable than new construction, but we still don't have the money."

"You might be able to get Edison Hardware to donate some of the materials. Or maybe get a crew together to work on reclaiming some wood and other materials from condemned properties in the area. I think there's a place up in Lawley that does that."

"Those are certainly options worth considering. I'm no stranger to drumming up donations. But I still doubt it would cover everything."

"You need a fundraiser."

It was the story of running a non-profit. "I'm sure we'd need several. The ones we've done in the past have barely been enough to manage the expenses of running what we already have. There's definitely never leftovers for building anything."

"So you need to think out of your original box. What about a calendar?"

"I've heard of other shelters doing that kind of thing. Everybody loves cute animal pics. But I have a hard time imagining that will raise enough to cover the cost of materials, let alone labor. The ones that make that kind of money usually involve hot guys."

"Like firefighters," he supplied.

"Yeah." She'd succumbed to a few of those herself from various causes she'd seen online over the years.

Hayden arched his brows, expectant. "You've got firefighters."

He was a firefighter. And apparently he was volunteering himself as eye candy. The idea of it made her grin. "I appreciate your willingness to help, Hayden, but I don't know that we'd sell out of a calendar full of you. Although I'd certainly buy one."

Clutching a hand to his heart, he adopted a piteous expression. "You wound me, madam." He sobered. "But no, not just me. I got a bunch of the other guys in the department to agree."

"You what?"

"After our conversation over breakfast, I sent a text out to the guys about the plight of the shelter. We've got a bunch of animal lovers who want to help."

Brooke stared at him, not quite believing what she was hearing. "You got an entire calendar's worth of guys from the fire department to volunteer to pose for a sexy calendar to raise money for the shelter?"

"Well, I don't know as I mentioned the sexy part. I figured we could pose with animals from the shelter. Maybe find homes for some of them while we're at it."

She'd shot down his initial attempt to solve her problem and he hadn't given up. Instead, he'd found another way to help, one that would, quite possibly, fund the entire endeavor. Sexy guys plus cute shelter animals would equal profits. Prospectively big ones if she could get a big enough social media campaign going. Her friend Cecily ran a marketing firm. She'd be all over that. But the idea had been Hayden's. He'd come to the rescue of her rescue…again. The fountain, it seemed, had worked overtime to grant her wish.

"You are amazing," she told him, sliding her arms around his shoulders.

Grinning, he tugged her closer. "I aim to please."

"Do you think they'd agree to something

on the sexier side? Because sexy sells."

"I'm reasonably sure we can talk them into it, as long as nobody is expected to lose their pants."

She snorted. It was a reasonable enough request, but she couldn't help messing with him, just a little. She arched a brow. "Nobody?"

His grin turned wicked. "I volunteer as tribute, as long as it's a private viewing."

Tipping her mouth up to his, she murmured, "I think we can work with that."

"OKAY PEOPLE!" Cecily Campbell, marketing genius, clapped her hands. "Let's get this show on the road. Where's our Mr. January?"

"Hey buddy, that's you." Hayden's firefighter buddy, Sean, had to actually kick him to drag his attention away from Brooke. In all fairness, Sean had his hands full of two kittens that were climbing from his arms to his fiancée, Delaney, and back again, so he didn't have a hand free to swat Hayden on the back of the head. "You're not jealous, are you?"

Brooke was talking to Zach Warren, the photographer who was donating his time to do this shoot for the rescue's fundraiser calendar. Hayden felt the tips of his ears getting warm and hot color flowing up the back of his neck. *Really missing my shirt right about now.*

Delaney laughed. "That's not jealous, that's besotted. He doesn't even see Zach."

"I'm going to go pose for this calendar now, since that's less embarrassing than talking to y'all," Hayden muttered as he walked away.

"Besotted." It fit. He wasn't embarrassed about his feelings for Brooke, it was more about being caught mooning after her, and having Delaney nail it like that didn't help. Neither did the fact that he was standing around in turnout pants and boots, suspenders chafing his bare nips. "Are you ready for your closeup, Miss Fluffington?"

The puppy in his arms rubbed her ear and yawned hugely. Halfway to Zach's staged area, Cecily took hold of Hayden's arm and starting tugging him forward like she thought he was going to run. Maybe she'd forgotten that he was the one who'd come up with this idea and had bribed, browbeaten, and guilt-tripped seventeen of his closest friends and fellow firefighters to pose for the eighteen-month calendar that would go on sale in July.

Maybe he had the look of a last-minute runner.

But if he looked nervous, it wasn't about being camera shy, or the thought of the Casserole Patrol and everyone else's granny asking him to autograph his half-naked picture. He had more important things on his mind. Next level things.

During the winter weeks, when the shelter had been temporarily relocated at the farm, Brooke had stayed on-site most nights. Because she'd felt a responsibility for the animals, but also because they'd been floating through those first heady weeks of a new relationship. He'd slid the rest of the way to head over heels in love with her over long talks in the barn, nights in sleeping bags, breakfasts in his kitchen.

Once the weather warmed enough, the kennels had been moved back to the rescue proper. Without having the animals at the farm, there hadn't been as many opportunities for sleepovers. They still spent as much time together as they could manage, but he'd missed that intensive one-on-one time over the past few months, missed her on those mornings he woke up without her. Hayden was hoping to do something about that today.

"You need to wake up, Princess Flufferina," he told the puppy in a low voice as Cecily left them. "Because after this, you've gotta help me carry out our plan, right?"

Hayden swung the puppy up to face him. The ball of white floof looked back at him with one brown eye, one blue. He'd scoped her out at the shelter when she'd arrived with three other siblings a couple weeks before. She'd taken one look at him and crawled into his lap for a nap. The double dew claws on her back feet said she was part Great Pyrenees, and Hayden was betting the other part was lab. She was a chillaxed puppy, and liked to snuggle into his chest without a bunch of scrabbling claws that would've scratched him up. He'd tried to resist, but every exposure had his willpower weakening. Two of her littermates had been adopted, and each visit he'd been relieved she was still there. Eventually he figured out what that meant.

"Okay, Hayden, time to get your cuddle on," Zach said.

Game for anything, Hayden followed all of Zach's instructions for posing, most of which involved just playing with the puppy while flexing his abs or arms or shoulders to show them at best advantage. It was hard to feel too much like meat when he had such an adorable ball of fuzz in his arms.

When he was finished, and it was Ben's

turn in front of the camera, Hayden wandered over toward the makeshift puppy corral where Brooke was overseeing things. She had that gleam in her eye, the matchmaking gleam that said more than one animal was going to find a forever home today.

He loved that look. He loved all her looks. He especially loved the smile that spread across her face when she caught him watching her.

He held his ground, wanting her to come to him, not wanting to have this conversation in the middle of the chaos of fur and firemen.

Brooke strode over, giving him a knowing smirk. "You know you want to keep her."

The puppy wasn't the only thing he wanted to keep. This was his moment. His stomach tightened as his heart kicked into gear. "Yeah. Yeah I do." Hayden held the puppy up to meet her gaze. "What do you think, Fluffbucket? You wanna come live with me?"

She licked his nose.

On a grin he turned his head as if she was

whispering in his ear. "What's that? You'll only come live here if your big buddy comes, too?"

He could see Brooke thinking through that, trying to sort out which other dog at the shelter he wanted to adopt. Tipping his head toward the puppy, he endured a wet Willy without breaking into laughter as he "listened" again. "Oh, you mean Tiny Tim *and* his mommy. I see."

Brooke's mouth dropped open, all traces of teasing gone. "Are you trying to coerce me into moving in with you by promising to adopt a puppy?"

Hayden fixed an innocent expression on his face and pointed to his chest. Maybe it was fast, maybe she wasn't ready for this step. He needed to keep things light. "Who, me? No. This is all Fluffernutter." He held the puppy up cheek to cheek with him. "I mean, can you really say no to this face?"

Her brows were knit. "Are you serious?"

He'd learned a lot about Brooke over the past months, including that sometimes her reserve just meant caution. She was a woman who needed to analyze all the angles, didn't just jump into things. So, he kept his tone casual, as if his heart wasn't pounding ninety to nothing against his sternum. "Yeah. Why not? You hate that your landlord won't let you have more than one animal. Tim loves it out here. So do you. Plus, think about how much faster you'll pay off your student loans not having to pay a fortune in rent."

"Those are all very practical reasons," she agreed.

"I know how much you value the practical." So he'd led with that, hoping it would make for a solid weight against the fact that this was all pretty fast. But maybe it was too fast. Maybe he should have waited for some kind of sign from her.

Or maybe...maybe he was thinking too much. Maybe the cute puppy play and the practical considerations weren't what she needed to hear.

Hayden tucked the puppy in his arm and

stepped into her space. He skimmed his fingers over the sun-warmed skin of her cheek, into her hair. "There's also the fact that I'm crazy about you."

She looked up at him, the serious expression giving way to that wide smile he adored as she slid her arms around him, sandwiching the puppy between them. "That's a better reason. It happens I'm crazy about you, too."

His heart gave a leap in his chest. "So is that a yes?"

She bent to press a kiss to the top of the puppy's head. "I don't know, what do you think, Flufferella?" Angling her head as if listening, she said, "You want to bring your brother? I don't know. Is that a dealbreaker?"

It wasn't fair. Hayden was so swamped with relief, he was a little lightheaded. Frankly, she could have asked for half a dozen dogs and he would have said yes just then. But he didn't care. The way he saw it, this was the first step in his master plan. Joint house and joint dogs led to joint life on a permanent basis. He was in a bit of a hurry; he could admit that. He knew it was fast, but he also knew it was right, and sometimes he wanted the rest of their lives to start. Right. Now.

But he could wait for more. He was learning he wasn't such a patient man where she was concerned, but he could wait for her to catch up. For now, he cuddled them both close. "I think that can be arranged."

Eyes sparkling, Brooke tipped her mouth up to his. "Then I guess you're getting a bunch of new roomies."

He kissed her, feeling the world spin just a bit, and then pulled her in close, knowing she'd be able to feel the hard thud of his heart that was still a little too fast. He bent his head, until his lips brushed the delicate shell of her ear. "Don't worry," he told her, soft and low, "you'll always be my favorite."

OTHER BOOKS BY KAIT NOLAN

A complete and up-to-date list of all my books can be found at https://kaitnolan.com.

THE MISFIT INN SERIES
SMALL TOWN FAMILY ROMANCE

- *When You Got A Good Thing* (Kennedy and Xander)

- *Til There Was You* (Misty and Denver)
- *Those Sweet Words* (Pru and Flynn)
- *Stay A Little Longer* (Athena and Logan)
- *Bring It On Home* (Maggie and Porter)

RESCUE MY HEART SERIES
SMALL TOWN MILITARY ROMANCE

- *Baby It's Cold Outside* (Ivy and Harrison)
- *What I Like About You* (Laurel and Sebastian)
- *Bad Case of Loving You* (Paisley and Ty prequel)
- *Made For Loving You* (Paisley and Ty)

MEN OF THE MISFIT INN
SMALL TOWN SOUTHERN ROMANCE

- *Let It Be Me* (Emerson and Caleb)

- *Our Kind of Love* (Abbey and Kyle)

WISHFUL SERIES
SMALL TOWN SOUTHERN ROMANCE

- *Once Upon A Coffee* (Avery and Dillon)
- *To Get Me To You* (Cam and Norah)
- *Know Me Well* (Liam and Riley)
- *Be Careful, It's My Heart* (Brody and Tyler)
- *Just For This Moment* (Myles and Piper)
- *Wish I Might* (Reed and Cecily)
- *Turn My World Around* (Tucker and Corinne)
- *Dance Me A Dream* (Jace and Tara)
- *See You Again* (Trey and Sandy)
- *The Christmas Fountain* (Chad and Mary Alice)
- *You Were Meant For Me* (Mitch and Tess)

- *A Lot Like Christmas* (Ryan and Hannah)
- *Dancing Away With My Heart* (Zach and Lexi)

WISHING FOR A HERO SERIES (A WISHFUL SPINOFF SERIES)
SMALL TOWN ROMANTIC SUSPENSE

- *Make You Feel My Love* (Judd and Autumn)
- *Watch Over Me* (Nash and Rowan)
- *Can't Take My Eyes Off You* (Ethan and Miranda)
- *Burn For You* (Sean and Delaney)

MEET CUTE ROMANCE
SMALL TOWN SHORT ROMANCE

- *Once Upon A Snow Day*
- *Once Upon A New Year's Eve*
- *Once Upon An Heirloom*
- *Once Upon A Coffee*

- *Once Upon A Campfire*
- *Once Upon A Rescue*

275

SUMMER CAMP
CONTEMPORARY ROMANCE

- *Once Upon A Campfire*
- *Second Chance Summer*

Kait is a Mississippi native, who often swears like a sailor, calls everyone sugar, honey, or darlin', and can wield a bless your heart like a saber or a Snuggie, depending on requirements.

You can find more information on this RITA ® Award-winning author and her books on her website http://kaitnolan.com. While you're there, sign up for her newsletter so you don't miss out on news about new releases!